Christmas at Holly Berry Inn

Emily C. Childs

Places to find Emily:

www.emilycauthor.com

Twitter: @echildsauthor

Facebook: https://www.facebook.com/emcchildsauthor/

Contents

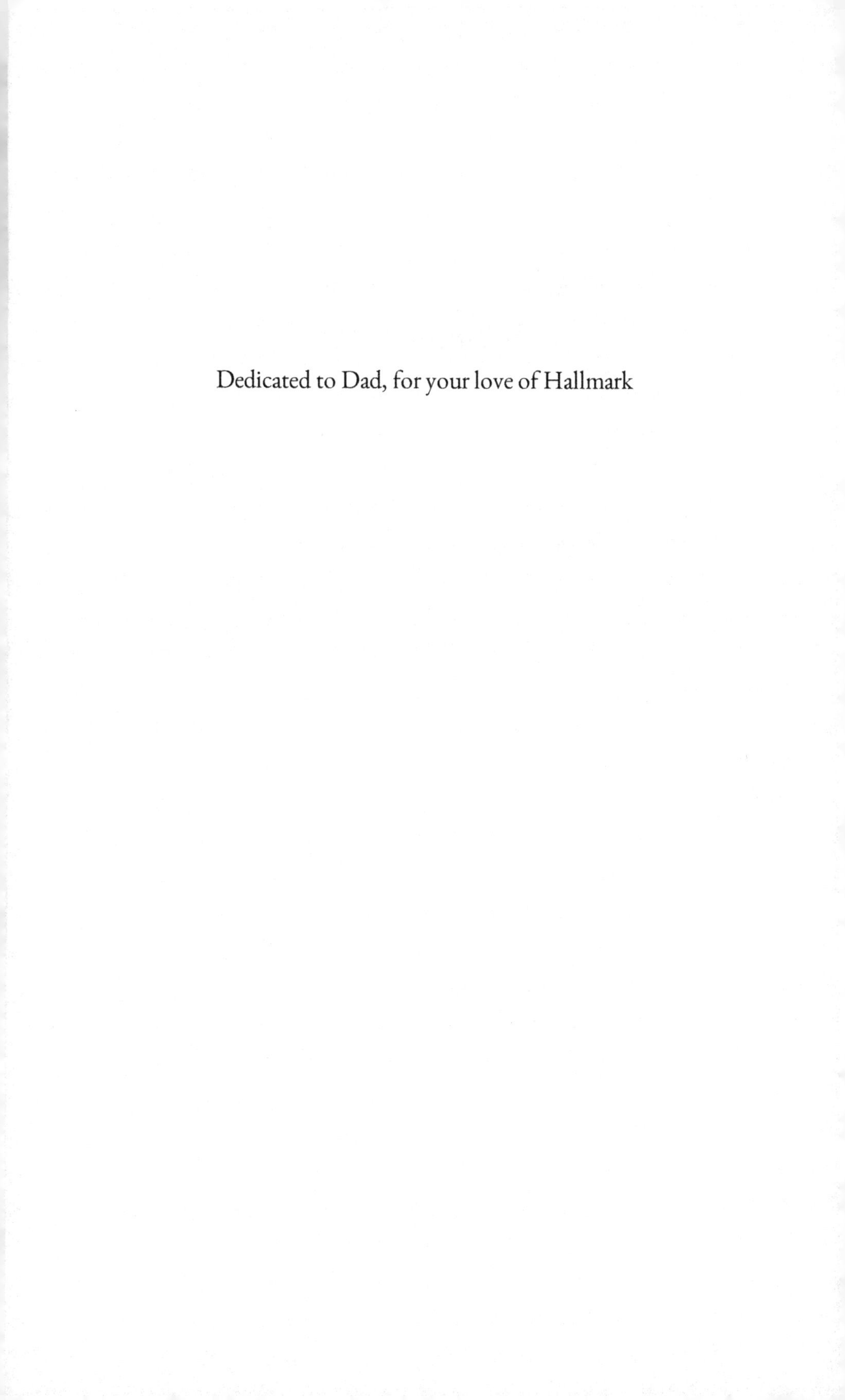

Dedicated to Dad, for your love of Hallmark

Christmas Present

Chapter 1

Sloan

The only thing I really like about this place are the smells. Ink and paper, vanilla and coffee. Luke reclines in his seat. I admit he pulls off the fitted suit amazingly well, but I'm still mad at him, and I make it clear by crossing my arms over my body, barring him out.

"We need a win on this, Sloan," he says with his milk chocolate smile. "With all the opposition given by the community, winning them over at the open house is top priority."

"Luke, you don't need to remind me. It'll be ready," I tell him, a little annoyed. He's had this conversation with me at least three times this week. What does he think I've been working on for the last eighteen months? "The lodge is ready, family friendly, and will be the best Christmas party that po-dunk town has seen in at least fifty years."

Luke chuckles. "There's the Sloan bite we all know and love."

I wince. He *used* to love it a little more.

Luke leans over his desk, his weight in his elbows. "Be careful, by the way. I don't like you staying at that motel—"

"It's an inn, well more like a B & B. I don't even think they have satellite, so I doubt there is much that can get me into trouble." I start to stand, hoping this conversation is over. I have a two-hour drive to make, and truth told, I don't want to be around Luke longer than I need to be. His little smirks, those green eyes, they are the sort of things a girl could get lost in, and I'm not going to fall for any of it again.

"Sloan you can cause trouble anywhere. It's what I've always liked about you." Luke laces his fingers behind his head and I hate it. The way his shirt sleeves roll up shows off the tone of his arms too well, and the relaxed top button leaves his tie a little loose and adds too much to the pinch in my chest.

I take a deep breath. Finish this project and I can move on from this place. He promised, and I have to believe this is as difficult for him to plaster fake smiles and easy talk as it is for me.

"Luke, I can handle an old guy at a bed and breakfast. Don't worry."

He scoffs and unlaces his fingers, but I'm satisfied enough when a bit of red tints his face. "Worried about you? No. You're too tough and no nonsense."

"Wow, you make me sound like a delight."

"You are." Heat darkens his eyes. "I know from experience."

My cheeks burn and I tighten my mouth. His sexy babble is not needed, nor welcome. "We don't need to go there," I whisper.

"Sorry," he holds up his hands in surrender. "Old habits."

My throat feels dry. It's still difficult to sit here, even after two months of being apart. There are too many memories of what we were in the spicy, clean scent of the cologne I bought him for his birthday, the picture of the California coast behind him from the vacation we took two summers ago, the way he looks at me as though he has so much to say, but never will.

I clear my throat as I gather my bag. "I still don't understand why I can't stay at the lodge. It's only fifteen more miles up the canyon."

"Plumbing is turned off," he tells me, and I think he should've probably led with that yesterday when he handed me my reservation at the Holly Berry Inn. "There was a problem on the third floor. Don't worry it'll be fixed by the open house."

"Luke," I say, shriller than before. "I am the property manager until the resort is open. You need to tell me when there is a problem on the property."

"I just did."

I am reminded all at once why we started fighting in the first place. "Yes, and it should've been my problem to deal with."

"You're mad I helped you out and took something off your list?"

"No," I say as I walk toward the door. "I'm upset you didn't discuss it with me. It's my job to handle the lodge."

"Most people would say thank you."

"Well, I'm not most people."

Luke laughs. "No, you're not."

"I better get going, it's supposed to snow. Anything else?"

Luke regards me for a long pause. I swear I see a flash of something like regret on his face, but soon enough it's buried underneath his cocky grin. He stands and crosses the office to me. This ought to be my cue to dip out, run for the hills—literally—and hideaway at the Holly Berry Inn until we're forced to socialize at the open house. But I freeze. He's too close, our shoulders brush.

"Be careful up there, Sloan," he says, voice husky. "And I wish you'd take me up on dinner sometime. I miss our dinners."

My tongue sticks to the top of my mouth. *Don't forget, Sloan.* "Yeah, well, maybe you could ask Kayla," I say in a tentative whisper. "If I recall you guys hit it off pretty good."

His grin fades. "How long are you going to punish me?"

My stomach feels as though a tight fist wraps around the middle. "I don't have a say in your life anymore, Luke. Let alone have the power to punish you. I need to go."

He shoves his hands in his pockets and takes a step back, the smooth, cool VP of Business for Bridger Ski and Sport returned. "Check in, Sloan. You will, won't you?"

"Yep, I'll be sure and let you know if the grouchy innkeeper pulls his shotgun on me."

"Not funny," he says over his shoulder, but he's grinning. "See you soon."

At that, I hurry out of the office. Back into the open floor of cubicles I free the breath I didn't know I'd been holding and rub the soreness in my chest. A few more weeks, and after New Year's I can transfer. I can have a new life. Mark Bridger already offered me a position on the management team at his Alpine resort in Utah. I can kiss Colorado goodbye and Luke with it.

When Mark brought the proposal of the new, private ski resort in Silver Creek Canyon, Luke jumped at the opportunity to run the business side. For three years he's done his job to epic proportions. But when Mark found out about my background in property management and with my MBA, well, soon enough I was in charge of the lodge and general store at the new resort. I wish I could tell that girl back then, the one who thought this was a sort of exciting adventure with her boyfriend, I wish I could tell her to open her naïve eyes. Maybe I can't blame Luke for the demise of us entirely. I've been entangled in the Lodge with hardly a day's break since they broke ground, then again, when he worked eighty-hour weeks at the beginning, I didn't seek the company of someone else.

I shake my head and lift my chin as I stride through the office. I don't need to think about Luke. What I ought to be worried about is spending a night at this hundred-year-old inn.

If I can tackle a multimillion-dollar lodge and ski resort project, I can certainly handle Old Bart, the crotchety old innkeeper, and if memory serves me right, he does keep a healthy dose of the worst sort of attitude.

I don't like rental cars. I drive a basic Honda and trying to figure out a four-wheel-drive SUV, while driving through a new snow burst makes me want to puke.

The road is already packed in fresh powder by the time I creep into Silver Creek. It looks so much like I remember, and a bit of nostalgia for easier days bites like the whipping breeze outside.

Despite my resume, sometimes I wonder if Mark Bridger agreed to hire me because I used to live here. I guess it doesn't matter. My work has proved itself enough to earn that permanent position at the Alpine resort. Still, it's strange being here.

White, twinkling Christmas lights wrap every old-fashioned lamp post. Evergreen bough garland shapes the windows and doorways of the shops: *Sam's Tool and Farm* hardware store, *Jones Market*, the one and only grocery store in town. I pause at the single stop light bobbing in the wind, and wait for the flash of green to guide me up the mountain pass toward the inn. Warming my hands, I take in the park. Even in the snow, the old place finally updated the playground into something not made of logs, old nails, and hot, metal slides. The library is on my opposite side, and I smile at the wide staircase leading into the old building. One of the largest places in town, and one of the oldest.

When the fighting grew too volatile at home, I'd slip in through the back door of the library with Rowan and binge the graphic novels, or fantasy books until reality faded into something magical.

We felt like little crooks, but really Rowan's grandma was the librarian up until the day she died. I'm pretty sure she knew exactly what we were up to since we often found canned soda or Doritos waiting for us on the return desk when we left.

I wince. I should've kept in touch with Rowan. We didn't leave things right. Then I roll my eyes. Like it matters. It's been eight years, and he doesn't live here anymore anyway. None of his family does, except for his grouchy great-uncle Bart. Yes, the innkeeper. Last I heard his mom and dad left, and since then only a few whispers on Facebook about the Graham family have found me over the years.

I shake my head. I don't want to think of the day my surest, strongest relationship went up in flames. Like a match to an open gas tank. At least the fallout felt a great deal like a massive explosion. I tighten my grip on the steering wheel. All I really want to do is finish this open house and leave Silver Creek. For good this time.

I've avoided the town for the most part during our work on the lodge. I've always gone the back way to the property. Silver Creek was my home from first grade to junior year. I'd roamed the sidewalks, buying penny candies from *Homer's Quik Stop*. I'd built snowmen on the school lawns and jumped off the bridge into the creek during the summer. I wonder if I would've stayed here if my family hadn't fallen apart.

Honestly, at this point, I doubt anyone here will remember me.

Turning off Main, I take the road that leads up the slope to Holly Berry Inn. They once held high school dances in the barn here, and our freshman year Rowan took me to one. I groan. So much for not thinking about him. We'd gone with our other friends, and didn't go to dance, not really, we went more to spy on older kids sneaking away to the stalls to do more than dance. Then we'd peg the handsy couples with acorns. We thought we were quite funny back then.

My tires slide on the final bend, and I slow to creeping pace. I think I top out at seven miles per hour when the fairy lights draping the old wrap-around porch come into view. A Victorian-style house with a turret on one side, and two double doors with painted glass on the front. The drive wraps around a small plot of spruce trees and ferns, and between them is a small wooden cottage with a hand-painted sign that says *Santa's Elf Hotel.* I smile. It is a little magical here, for families at Christmas, I suppose. The barn is glowing, the wash of light spills over the corrals and pastures where guests can ride horses in the Spring and Summer. A big hit when hunters come for deer season.

The roof is lined in gold lights, the banisters in green and red.

I hesitate to leave the warmth of the car, but Bart won't like anyone checking in after nine o'clock. With a bit of reluctance, I park in one of the guest stalls by the wooden fence and gather my bag. Snow falls in puffy flakes, sticking to my lashes, smearing my makeup before I even get to the porch.

A cheery bell announces my arrival and inside I'm blasted with a wave of warm air, a rustic smell, like burning firewood and a hint of cinnamon.

The front desk is empty apart from a desktop computer, a messy stack of papers, and a covered plate of reindeer shaped sugar cookies. The rough-cut wood floor groans with each step, but I crack a smile.

Someone has given this old place some love since last I saw it.

The once cluttered shelves are now decorated in appropriate moose or wooden bears. Bart always had the hearth and shelves littered in odds and ends, like old books or farm tools that did nothing but gather dust. The log chairs in the front lobby are accented in sweet throw pillows or thickly knitted afghans, and the drapes aren't the old, yellowed daisy curtains anymore. A basic forest green, that I'm sure serve as black-out shades for guests who care to sleep beyond sunrise.

I take a full turn around the front, and startle when a chipper voice at my back says, "Hi! Want a room?"

I whip around and am met with a gummy grin, missing two front teeth, and pigtails. A girl, she can't be older than eight, beams at me with thick-framed purple glasses.

"Hi," I say with a grin. I have no idea who this kid is, but she's got a smile for days. "Um, yes. I have a reservation."

"Great," she says and faces the computer.

"They seem to be working you hard," I say, leaning back to peek into the large living room for a glimpse of an adult lifeform.

She giggles. "What's your name?"

"Uh . . ." Is a kid really going to check me in? "Sloan Hanson."

The little girl uses the mouse to scroll for half a heartbeat. "Hmm, there is an S. H. but the reservation is from Bri-Brigger—"

"Bridger Ski Resort?" I help her out.

"Yeah," she says, beaming again.

"That's me."

She double clicks with the mouse, and squeaks a bit of pleasure. "Okay. One night it is."

I make kind of huff when she prints out a receipt and asks me to sign. "Huh, impressive service."

"Have a cookie," she says. "And if you get asked maybe you can tell my —"

"Abigail."

I stop signing at the rumbling voice. The girl's eyes widen, but she hurries and whispers, "Tell him I did good, then he'll give me the job."

"Sorry about that, she likes to think we run a sweatshop here and hire eight-year-olds."

"I'm nine in January," she pouts.

I chuckle and turn around as I say, "Actually, she was very professional, I think you might want to consider—"

I stop midsentence. Standing a foot from his broad shoulders, I meet his coffee colored eyes. He furrows his brow, but there is a flash of heat in his gaze. Surprise? Anger?

It doesn't matter that his face is covered in a dark beard now, or that he's wearing a tattered baseball cap. It doesn't even matter that he's grown into something like a giant, what is he—six foot four? I'd still know him.

I swallow past the thick knot in my throat, palms sweaty. My voice comes out all wrong, breathy and raw when I whisper, "Rowan?"

Chapter 2

Rowan

"Rowan?"

I hear her, but a response is stuck somewhere between my brain and the back of my throat. I don't really notice much of anything. Not the way Abigail is looking at me like I've lost my mind, I don't even hear the stupid *Noel Playlist* the kid insists must be cyclical for the entire month of December.

All I can do is stare. Like an idiot. Like I'm fifteen again, fumbling over my words and stupid feet.

She tilts her head, pale eyes are narrowed. There are some people from the past you think on both warmly and bitterly. Well this woman, she does that in spades.

"Sloan Hanson," I say, slowly. I clear my throat and take a decent step backward.

Sloan shakes her head. She wears her hair long now, and it's darker than I remember, but she still has those thick, black lashes that are long enough to touch her brow.

"What are . . . what are you doing here?" she asks. "I mean, what happened to Bart?"

"He's moved to an old person's colony in Arizona," Abigail chirps.

"It's not a colony, Abs," I say, forgetting Sloan is standing there and break a smile. "He's not a honeybee."

"Huh." Sloan takes a deep breath and faces the front desk again.

Abigail hands over a keycard, beaming. "Here is your key, *Ma'am*," she exaggerates with a glance at me. "Enjoy your stay."

"Thanks," Sloan says hurriedly. She rummages through that enormous shoulder bag, but gives up for whatever she's after and cautiously takes a step toward me. "I have . . . excuse me," she says. "More bags."

I stand aside when she points toward the door, and I watch her leave into the blizzard.

Abigail clears her throat and gives her glasses a decent nudge when they slip down her nose. She's pointing at the door.

I shrug. "What?"

She rolls her eyes. "Go help."

"You don't work here, bossy," I say in my best I'm-in-charge-of-you-voice. "Now, go do your math sheet."

Outside the wind takes my breath away. I tug my coat collar up under my jaw, grumbling about the plowing I'll need to do in an hour if we're going to keep the door swinging. Sloan is leaned over the backseat of a black SUV. I scoff, her boots are high heels. The woman was born in the snow, and lived here plenty long to know better.

Sloan Hanson. I'm still a little stunned. And how did she recognize me so quickly? I'm making a good effort to embrace mountain-man grunge, I wear steel-toed boots, and flannel coats. Hardly the twiggy, squeaky-voiced kid who got into arguments about Palpatine and Darth Vader back then.

Sloan drags out a wheeled suitcase from the seat and grunts when it plops like dead weight into the snow.

"Need help?" I fight a smile when she startles.

"Geez," she says. "I didn't even hear you." She blinks rapidly through the sheets of snow, then pulls up the handle of her bag as though it might beat the impossible and wheel through the snow. "I'm good."

I snort and take the bag out of her hand. "Abigail insisted."

Sloan tugs a knitted snow hat over her wet hair, and there is a twitch in the corner of her mouth. "Well, in that case."

We make the wet walk toward the house, she hugs her coat tightly around her body. Truth told, part of me thinks she's guarding herself from me. The feeling is mutual. I don't want to get too close because this is a little surreal, a little uncomfortable.

"She's cute," she says.

I open the door when we stomp the snow off our boots. "Who?"

"The kid."

"Abby?"

"Yeah. She's cute. Who is she? Can't be yours; I think I'd remember if you had a kid. I mean unless she's someone else's who . . . you're close . . . to." She clears her throat and turns away like she's embarrassed.

How did we let this connection between families die? I don't know if I'm more bitter at Sloan for being so distant and cut off or at me for keeping it this way. "Oh, yeah. She's cute, and my niece. But I'm her guardian."

Sloan stops abruptly, like I've punched her in the gut. "Jenny's?"

My jaw tightens. "Yep."

"I-I didn't know—"

I drop her bag at the entrance and point at the staircase. "It's fine. The room is on the third floor. Sorry, no elevator. Jericho has breakfast ready as early as seven each morning in the dining room."

"Rowan . . ."

"I've got a few things to do, are you good from here?" I don't want to do this, dredge up the old wounds. I don't want to talk about how my best friend fell off the face of the earth because of the things I said, or how I turned into someone she wouldn't recognize after she left. I don't want to admit how it felt to reach out a couple years back, only to have those pathetic, maybe a little drunken, requests go unanswered.

"Yeah," she says quietly. "Yeah, I'm good."

I offer a brisk nod, and leave quickly to the kitchen where a kid better be working on her homework. I strip off my coat, too hot all at once. My head is in a sort of spin, as though in a fog. For years in high school, friends teased me for keeping Sloan's pictures on my phone, the way I talked about her like she'd come back. Back when I ran my mouth and broke her heart, I guess I thought it would blow over since we'd practically lived every day together for a solid decade, but that's life. It sucks sometimes, then reels back around and slaps you in the face with reminders that it does.

Sloan Hanson is here.

I crack my thumb knuckles and slip into the kitchen. "Hey kid," I say to Abigail. She's hunched over a worksheet with an owl holding math facts at the top. I point at the doodle she's working on with great focus. "What's this? Doesn't look like you're multiplying."

She pouts. "You're supposed to time me."

Oh, now I understand the hesitation. "Hey," I say as I slip out my phone. "Remember what we talked about. As many as you can do is enough, Abs."

She starts coloring the owl with her pencil. "I can't do it."

"Yes, you can."

She gives a sort of whiney groan, and her knee bounces under the table. Before the melt down comes, I nudge her arm. "Deal time." My niece's face brightens, enough that I laugh. "I won't time you with the stopwatch."

"Really?" she asks with a touch of hesitation. The rules are timed math facts, and there is one thing Abigail hates most—not following her teacher's rules. But she's intrigued, and follows my hand as I reach for a plate of leftover sugar cookies.

"Really," I tell her. "Instead, let's see how many you can get done by the time I finish this Santa cookie."

Her face twists and she peeks at me over the rims of her glasses when they slip down her nose. I make a note to take her into Doc Heart and get them adjusted. Abigail's face is flushed and she stares at her math sheet timidly.

I lift the cookie to my lips and wink. "Ready?"

Abigail holds her breath, but presses her pencil to the paper.

"Go!" I take the first bite and she's off. Knees bouncing under the table, her tongue out one side of her mouth. She keeps checking on my progress as she goes through her times tables. One line is finished by the time the Santa's hat is gone, and when he's nothing but a torso she's starting on the third.

"And done," I say, brushing crumbs from my hand.

Abigail drops her pencil. I guess I expected her to laugh and love this new system, but, as usual, she looks at me with those big hazel eyes, and shudders to keep the tears away.

"I got three . . . three less," she says, voice wavering.

I close my eyes and sigh. "You did great Abs."

"I'm trying!" Now the tears come. "I *promise*, I'm trying."

My stomach feels as if a fist curls around my insides, twisting in something hot and angry as I gather her little body in my arms and pull her against my chest. "Abigail—"

"I'm sorry, Uncle Ro."

My mouth goes tight and I'd like to put a hole through the wall. Instead, I keep her head under my chin, and nudge her math sheet toward me. I take a moment to review her answers then squeeze her. "You actually got more."

She sniffs and pulls back. "What?"

"Yeah, you only missed one," I say with a smile. "You missed five last time. Kiddo, that means you did better than last night."

There it is the faintest hint of a smile in the corner of her mouth. "Really?"

"Really."

Another breath shudders out of her throat and her shoulders visibly slouch as she relaxes. "But I still need to do better. Grant, he sits next to me, he finishes the entire sheet. Every. Time. I'll do better." By now she's talking to herself, not me anymore.

I bump her shoulder with mine and hand her a reindeer cookie. "You know what, even if you didn't, then that just means we try again tomorrow night. Do a few math problems change how much you matter where it counts?" I press a hand to my heart.

Her eyes go misty, but she cracks that toothy smile and shakes her head. "Nah," she says. "We're a team."

We bump fists. "That's right, we're a team, and teammates help each other. We don't hurt each other." When she giggles as I draw a big smiley face on her paper, I feel like no matter what has happened to bring us here, I'd live to keep this girl laughing. "Alright, shower time, stinky."

"I don't stink."

"Eh, I don't know. Hurry up, Nana and Pops are calling soon."

She practically hops off her chair and bounces up the stairs. I smile as she goes, but over my knees, beneath the table, my fists clench. *Jenny,* I think, *I'm trying, but man, I wish you were here.*

"Bye Nana!" Abigail chirps at the phone screen. My mom blows a kiss and promises to drop a dump truck filled with presents on her head when they come for Christmas.

"Go hop into bed, kiddo," I say. "Start reading, and I'll be there in a sec."

Abigail starts to whine, but thankfully, when Nana tells her to listen good or it'll just be a wagon full, she again bounds up the stairs singing a mix of *Up on the Housetop* and *Jingle Bells.*

"That girl," my mom says when it's my turn to look at the screen. "She is just a gem. How are you doing, Ro?"

"We're good," I say.

"Honey—" My mom sounds exactly like that—a mom. As if I'm not a grown twenty-five-year-old guy. "You can be real with me," she goes on. "I raised two children. I know it's not all peaches and cream."

The one thing about the Graham family is we learned at a young age that feelings, even the crappy ones, were better served in the open. Jenny and I teased our parents relentlessly for their little hippie-kumbaya communication circles forced upon us as soon as we formed words. I sigh and check to make sure Abigail isn't hiding on the stairs, then turn back to my mom. "Her anxiety is still there, and I don't know if I'm helping or making it worse." I dig into the issue with her timed math facts, but it's not really about the math. By the end, heat prickles up the back of my neck. "Scott . . . he just did a number on her, and I wish I could—"

"That won't help her," Mom says. "You getting angry and saying things that'll hurt her, even if they're said with the best intentions." Mom rubs the bridge of her nose. "I wish I could be there, for you both. Sometimes I feel so guilty—"

"Mom," I interrupt. "You and Dad help, and these calls mean everything to her. Abs knows you guys are in her corner, but Dad needs you right now."

I can tell my mom wants protest, but I'm right, and she knows it. Since my dad got sick, his lungs simply can't handle the altitude up here. When blue became a normal color to his lips, doctors insisted if they didn't move to lower elevations, breathing would be like a constant knife to his chest. Still, moving away from me, from Abigail, I don't know if I've ever seen my mother cry that much.

My mom smiles with a bit of sadness. "Thanks, Ro. I'm proud of you. For how you stepped in these few years, for us, and for Abby. I hope you realize the way you've changed her life. Jenny, she'd be so . . ." She hiccups. "Well, she'd give you the biggest hug, you know the kind, the ones she always gave that felt like she'd break your neck."

We laugh, and the familiar ache blooms in my chest, like I want to hold my breath until it starts to burn. We talk a bit more about Dad and how he'll be during Christmas. They insist on staying until New Year's and when my Dad shows up on the screen I make him promise he won't pretend like he can snowshoe or ski like he used to.

"How's business?" he asks when my mom runs to take something out of the oven.

"Last week we were booked with a ski team. They came to be the first runs on the new private resort."

"Ah, right," Dad says. "I still think it'll change the town, all those exclusive folks coming in."

I laugh. My dad is a good ol' boy from a small town. Nice as he is, I think the man will always be wary of those who move into Silver Creek with their big city ideas. "It's not bad for the town. They spend their money here, so it'll be good, I think. And, like last week, it brings business to me. I'm not the one at county meetings complaining about growth and change."

"Sell out," Dad says with a smile.

"Speaking of guests," I say and clear my throat even thinking about her. "You'll never guess who showed up with a reservation tonight."

My mom pokes her head back into the frame. "Who?"

I snort. It's like the woman can taste gossip. She's a busybody, but I'm not sure I'd have made it through the last five years without her bracing our entire family on her back. I lower my voice. "Sloan Hanson."

I'd say it again to watch my mom's eyes go wide as if they might pop out of her head. "You are kidding me. Sloanie?" I hear my mom slap her coffee table when I just nod. "Well, don't leave it there, Rowan. Tell me about her. Why is she there? What's her life like now? Oh, how is her mom? I haven't talked to Kris in, geez, at least a year."

"Mom, cool it," I say, laughing. "Honestly, I didn't know you talked with Kristine anymore."

"Mostly on birthdays. That's the good thing about Facebook, I guess. So, tell me about Sloan. You two were the biggest peas in a pod. I still think Sloan was the only friend we allowed sleepovers with."

"Yeah, a co-ed. What were my parents thinking?" I smile, and do remember the many campouts with Sloan in my backyard. We were Abigail's age, so it was all innocent, until the random campout at thirteen. Probably not the best idea for new teenagers. Nothing happened or anything, it's just the night I noticed that my best friend was a *girl* and one who started causing all kinds of sick twists in my gut. I didn't get it then, but that's when sleepovers stopped.

"Rowan."

My mom's voice drags me back to the conversation. "What? Sorry."

"What's she like? Why is she there?"

"Mom, I don't know. We said maybe five words to each other. She had no idea I bought the Inn from Bart and I think we were both a little surprised."

My mom rolls her eyes. "I'll expect a much, *much* better report tomorrow night."

"Maybe I'll just let her talk to you," I say. I'm teasing but my mom pauses as if it's a decent suggestion. No way. "Hey, I've got to go put Abs to bed. Talk to you guys tomorrow, okay."

"Give her kisses for us!" Mom says.

"Which one? Sloan or Abigail?" my dad chimes in.

"Funny, Dad. Really, you're getting quicker."

"It's what I'm here for."

It takes another minute to hang up and get upstairs. I creep past the locked door that shares the hallway with Abigail. My throat feels dry as I shove my hands into my pockets and hurry past, grateful Sloan Hanson has a reservation for one night.

I'm anxious to get back to normal, and back to pretending after all this time she doesn't still make my head spin.

Chapter 3

Sloan

The sun isn't up, but I'm awake, staring aimlessly at the ceiling. I'm not sure how long I slept, if I even fell asleep at all.

Rowan Graham.

All those reminiscent thoughts while driving through town, if I were more philosophical I might think I manifested him back into my life. Rowan left town. He'd joined the Army for crying out loud, how could I have anticipated he'd be the one who owned the Holly Berry Inn?

Yet here he is.

All rugged and brooding and silent. After all this time, after how he ended things, I'd expect at least an apologetic glance. My jaw tightens. If he's still pouting about how things went with us, well, it's about time he let it go. No sense holding on. It's not as though I mattered that much to him—a notion he made crystal clear right before I moved away.

I don't think we should talk anymore. It'll be easier. Kind of like a band aid goodbye.

That's what he'd whittled our years-long friendship too. A band aid.

I dig the heels of my palms into my eyes as if I can blot out the memory. Seventeen is hard enough, and it took some doing, but eventually I used those last words to grow a bit stronger. Certainly, I learned to keep intimate thoughts private.

Maybe I took it a bit far. Luke once told me getting any sort of sweet nothing out of my mouth was like speaking to the dead and expecting a long-winded response.

A big letdown.

Sounds harsh, I know, but he wasn't wrong. It took me two years to say the big I love you to Luke, then eight months later, I was again reminded why it's better to keep those silly confessions inside when I caught him with Kayla.

I kick off my sheets. It's not even seven, but I'm more than anxious to leave. My chest is tight and my neck aches. I must've clenched all night. I rummage through my toiletry bag and take out the chamomile and lavender cream, running it over my hands and inhaling until I feel a little calmer, a litter more revived.

I hurry and shower, do my makeup, and ignite my curls until the hazelnut waves bounce around my shoulders. I'd like to get to the lodge by nine at the latest to start knocking out my checklist of all things needing to be addressed before the open house.

I slip into my stylish burgundy sweater with faded jeans, never pausing between tasks. If I do, then the cramp in my chest will blossom into an ache, maybe even pain. There is part of me that wants to talk with Rowan about things that happened, wants to hash out our last conversation, maybe apologize for starting something right when Jenny died. He hadn't needed my silly lovesick confession, no, he'd needed a friend who understood him. The one who knew he'd need to hike in silence, or stare at the stars, simply being still.

He knew books, and popcorn, and old movies distracted me from the storm behind the Hanson's closed doors. I close my eyes. We just . . . knew things.

And now we're strangers.

"Stop it," I say out loud as I finish zipping my ankle boots. I'm leaving today, and we can pretend like this never happened.

Warm smells of sausage, toast, and coffee float up the stairs as I quietly carry my suitcase down. I don't want to disturb any other guests, and would like to check out without much hold up, or awkward goodbyes.

When a blur of laughter, snow boots, and braids whizzes past, I nearly stumble back on the stairs.

"It's a snow day!" Abigail pauses to inform me.

I smile and nod, basking in her joy for a moment. Until I look outside. My mouth drops. At least four feet of fresh powder blankets the front drive. I can't even see the cute, little Santa's Elf house anymore. Snow packs around my SUV, hiding the tires, and crushing the top. I press my face against the window, inspecting the front porch. It's halfway shoveled, but there is still a bank pressed against the front door that is more like an ice wall than anything.

"Snow day!" Abigail rounds back. Now she is zipping up a puffy coat. "No school."

"Lucky you," I tell her. My eyes sting. I can see Jenny in the girl's eyes. "Hey, you checked me in so awesome last night, do you know how to check me out? I think I better start sweeping my car off so I can get on my way."

"Only ATVs and snow plows are going anywhere this morning."

I glance over my shoulder and catch the eye of a curvy woman with curly dark hair tied low on her neck. She has a red polo with the Holly Berry logo on the breast, and beams over a tray of cinnamon rolls. Those catch my eye since the frosting is still oozing over the warm bread.

"But I need to get up the canyon."

She chuckles. "Yeah, sorry. That's not going to happen. The upper canyon is completely closed for at least a couple days."

My eyes widen. I glance at my watch. It's early, and I have hope none of the employees at the lodge are there without plumbing. If it closed last night, they'd be safely at home. Still, I ought to call and check. If anyone is stranded up there, I'm the manager of the place, I'd need to arrange a way to get to them.

After I think all that, thoughts turn a bit woeful and are rife in self-pity.

"I need to get to the Moosehead Lodge. It's really important."

The woman's smile fades a little and she gestures out the window. "Girlfriend, do you see what's happening outside?" Then she winks at Abigail. "It's like the entire North Pole came to stay with us."

The little girl beams, showing off the gap in her smile, and hurries to the window, bouncing on the window seat.

My jaw tightens. I know exactly what Luke will say. Ugh, I can hear his tone already: *Thought you wanted this, Sloan. You think a guy like Mark got to where he is because he stopped at some snow. We're in the middle of the Rockies, opening a ski resort. There's bound to be snow.*

Maybe it won't be word for word, but that'll be the gist.

"I have four-wheel drive." I'm talking more to myself, but the woman with the cinnamon rolls snorts and I'm pretty sure she says, "Good luck" as she leaves to the dining room.

"You can stay another night with us," Abigail chirps, delightfully oblivious to the strained expression on my face.

"Thanks," I say, "but I have a really important meeting I've got to get ready for up the canyon."

"It'll be fun. It's Wednesday and we always make pizza on Wednesday."

I grin. "I thought pizza was meant for Fridays."

"Uncle Ro says we made it halfway through the week," she tells me as she glides on her mittens and readies to brave the blizzard. "So we deserve fun food. But . . . he says that about Friday and Sunday too."

She glances at me, perplexed.

I laugh, but there's an ache in my gut. Now that she mentions it, Rowan memories usually came with some sort of excuse to get pizza in all its forms: pizza sticks, pizza rolls, pizza pie, fruit pizza. I guess some things don't change.

Abigail buttons the top of her coat. "Well, I'm going to go outside."

"Don't get lost in the snow."

She plops a too-big knit cap over her head. The tail ends in a fluff ball and hits the small of her back. "I'm going to be on my sled."

A drift of snow flurries into the inn when she leaves, and I'm alone. I drum my fingers over the front desk, waiting for someone to take my key. Hopefully, it isn't Rowan, then again, part of me hopes it is. After a minute or two of waiting, I make my way into the dining room, unable to hold back from the smells of breakfast.

The woman with curly hair is tipping mugs onto saucers on the few tables. A man is tucked in one corner, still in his flannel pajamas as he stares at the screen of his laptop. At the center table a couple snuggles close together, smiling as if they're sickeningly happy.

"Ah, decided you're hungry," the woman calls to me.

I weave my suitcase through the tables and go to where she's now placing a silver cooking tray filled with scrambled eggs onto a warmer. "Listen, Miss, uh—"

"Jericho," she says. I take a guess that she's maybe thirty, give or take a year or so. "The genius behind the food at this old place. You can call me Jeri."

"Jeri, everything looks great, but I just need to check out and no one is up front."

"Still on that? I doubt you'd even be able to pull out of the parking lot. Really, stay awhile. The Prentises are staying an extra night." She points a set of tongs at the couple and lowers her voice to a whisper. "But they're on their honeymoon, so I doubt they care to go anywhere really."

"Trust me," I tell her. "I don't want to go out in the storm, but I'm the property manager for the new resort—"

She whistles softly. "Ritzy place."

I grin, taking that as a compliment, even if I can't quite tell if she's for or against the new resort. At the county council meetings, Luke told me, the town is a bit mixed. "Yeah," I say. "It's nice. But we have a big open house on Christmas Eve and there is a to-do list a mile long. I really can't delay getting there."

Jeri doesn't seem pleased, even adds a dramatic little huff. "Well, you're a grown woman. I'll make sure your checkout is all done up in neat bow. But you've at least got to take a cinnamon roll for the road. I guarantee they'll bring you back to stay here."

Doubtful, but I smile and take one in a Styrofoam container as I hand over my key. I thank her and take a wide berth around the newlyweds who can't keep their mouths off each other and dare the outdoors.

The air cuts through my coat like sewing pins all along my skin, and my nose sticks together with every breath I draw in. I glance warily at the rental SUV and swallow. It'll take some doing to brush off the snow on top, but I notice a line of push brooms against the porch. I have a feeling the line of bristles stand at attention waiting for days as this. Taking one, I trudge through the snow that if the drive weren't plowed, it would hit my knees.

My suitcase sinks into the snow as I start sweeping off the snow block on the roof and windshield. Every finger is stiff when I peel my frozen grip from the broomstick. Maybe my ears froze because I don't hear the rumble of the four-wheeler, complete with a heavy-duty plow on the front, stop next to the car.

"What do you think you're doing?"

I whip around as Rowan hops off the seat, brushing thick flakes off his snow beanie.

"Going to work. At the new lodge," I shout over the noise of his machine and point deeper into the canyon.

"You are not," he grumbles as he snatches the broom from my hand. "Not even the plows can get up there."

"Well, I'm not a rookie when it comes to driving in the snow."

"Yeah, I don't think snowplow drivers are rookies either."

I forget to breathe. He peers down at me, eyes like hot coals. Rowan is breathtakingly tall. His arms aren't the lanky limbs attached to his body they once were, and I'm ashamed to admit I wouldn't mind if I ever became reacquainted with how those arms felt around me again. Rowan was never afraid of hugging me, other people, maybe. But we knew how to embrace. Whether we did it to bug each other or if it was sincerely needed. Now, he crosses his arms, staring at me like I'm a pest that needs to be squashed. But one he doesn't want to see get in the car at the same time.

"I need to go," I tell him. "I don't have a choice."

"You'll wreck."

"Thanks for your concern, Rowan, but I'll be fine." I say, a little snidely. I slip past him and working my way to the driver's side, then toss my wet suitcase in the back, and look forward to blasting the heater until my feet dry again. "Good to see you again."

I let out a squeak when the driver's door slams shut as I am about to get in. Rowan has his hand on the door, and he's, well, he's glaring. Like I've slapped him and he has a lot to say about it.

"You're not going up the pass, Sloan."

Uh . . . what? The air is cold, but heat floods my cheeks. I narrow my eyes until I can hardly see through my snowflake-covered lashes. "Last I checked, I'm not your property and can do as I please."

Then like a toddler he slips in front of the door, blocking it with his giant body. I use my shoulder to try to shove him away. "Rowan, move."

"Nope."

"Oh, my gosh. Are you five? Move."

"I can't, in good conscience, let a guest leave when their brain isn't working."

"And you also can't keep someone against their will. Now, move."

He glares at me, but there is a twitch in the corner of his mouth. I could strangle him. He's loving this. Rowan takes off one glove, fiddles with his cell phone, then flashes the weather app in my face. There are traffic cameras in the canyon, and he shows me an image taken two minutes before. It's a total whiteout.

"You're not going, Sloan."

"Step aside, Rowan," I warn.

Like he's had a bit of practice, Rowan snatches the keys from my gloved hands.

"Hey!" I bounce and try to snatch them. "Give those . . . Rowan Birk Graham."

His eyes widen. "Middle name is off limits on this property."

"Oh, I'll start shouting deeper secrets than your middle name if you don't *give me those keys.*" I make a swipe for them but slip when it's hard miss.

Rowan catches me before I land on my back. And all at once those arms are around me. My pulse won't stop racing. The roof of my mouth is sticky, and I swallow too loudly. Rowan's bitter coffee eyes break into me for a heartbeat. Focused and thoughtful, the boy I once knew.

His voice is low rasp. "You're staying, Sloan. I know you aren't that stupid to go up there."

Hardly the sweet things such a moment demands, and I am tossed back into the bleak reality which has built a steely wall between us. Shoving him back, I don't mean to blurt out the words, but I'm mad enough I could smack him. They simply spill out. "Don't pretend you know me at all. You don't, not anymore."

Awkward silence follows, the kind that I'll stew over in the middle of the night two or three years from now. When I can't stand the way he channels his scrutiny, I rip out my suitcase from the back seat and start the trek back to the inn. "I'm calling CDOT, you lunatic." The Department of Transportation will know when roads will open, and it better be soon. I don't know what I'll do if it's not, probably eat my cinnamon roll times five more in one sitting, or something equally dramatic. I spare him an angry glance over my shoulder. "Do you hold all your guests hostage? On second thought, maybe I ought to call the cops."

"Give them a call, they're regulars on Thursdays for Jeri's homemade hot chocolate and pumpkin bread," he says.

"Just . . . let's not talk," I mutter, and I don't think he heard over the engine of his four-wheeler. He's impossible. Smug, arrogant, grumpy, maybe a little sexy too, and I hate that my mind insists on adding the last part. This is Rowan. Knife-to-my-heart Rowan Graham. He doesn't deserve the satisfaction of my attention.

The front door slams at my back, and I shudder when the blast of heat inside the inn chases the chill away almost too swiftly.

"Welcome to the Holly Berry Inn," Jeri chirps as she puts out new sugar cookies. Snowflakes and mistletoe this time. She's beaming at me, and I know she recognizes me, so clearly she's teasing. "Here's your key."

I roll my eyes and snatch the key out of her hand. I doubt she even officially checked me out of the inn.

"Glad Rowan got my message." She's trying not to laugh.

"Seriously?" I gape. "You had to sic the guard dog on me?"

"Hey, he said you knew him and told me to keep an eye on you. Just looking out for my new girl." She nudges my shoulder and giggles.

"Keep an eye on me?"

"So what's the history?" Jeri goes on, ignoring me. "How do you know each other?"

I shoot a broken-glass glare at the window where Rowan is riding back and forth, shoveling snow. "We *don't*." He ignores me, acts like I'm the plague who rushed back into his life, then has the nerve to put eyes on me, trap me, and treat me like I belong to him.

I'll admit I didn't expect my heart to break.

How long did I want Rowan's attention, his voice on the other line? The guy who I loved like a friend, and a little more, behaves like I'm a regret that a blizzard is keeping in his life. So he'll keep watch on me via surrogate. Never needing to really talk to me except taking me hostage in a parking lot. I should be angry, the delirious kind, but it hurts more than anything.

I point at Jeri, refusing to show that I actually like her. She's one of those humans that you can't help but gravitate toward and enjoy her company. But I make my voice take on a growly tone. "You picked the wrong side."

"Well, he is my boss."

I lean over the counter, one brow raised, a sly grin on my lips. "And I know a slew of embarrassing, I'm talking life-changing, stories."

Jeri plays along and rests her chin on her hands. "This just got saucy. Are you really poaching me to your side of a lover's quarrel? I'm flattered."

"Lover's quarrel, no," I say easily. "Rowan Graham is officially my enemy."

"Even better."

I shrug. "You picked the grump outside, though."

"Oh, girl, I'm on your side. Woman power and all. But I'm still not sold on what kind of battle we've got going on. See, I've never been asked to keep watch on a guest, and I've never seen a guest keep stealing glances at the said grump like you are."

Am I? I take a quick inventory and do find I am leaning in such a way that I can peek outside as often as I want. I clear my throat, keeping my grin in place. "Trust me, if you're looking for romance, you're not finding it with me and that guy."

She laughs again and closes the cookie case. "We'll see. Hey, since the road is closed into town for the next few hours, I'm putting a simple soup and salad buffet out for lunch."

"Sounds great," I tell her and start the trek back to my room.

"Hope you enjoy the rest of your stay," Jeri says, a gleam in her eyes. "I know I'll enjoy watching the next few days."

She'll need to enjoy glares and biting comments then because that is all Mr. Rowan Graham will be getting from this face, ever.

Chapter 4

Rowan

"Hey, it's time to start pizza, or are you avoiding us in here?"

I stop hacking at the wood on the cutting block and turn around. "Be there in a second, Jeri."

She grins and hugs her coat tightly around her body. The snow is easing up, but a slide took out a piece of the upper canyon road. It'll be blocked for at least two days. No doubt Sloan will take that news as gracefully as she took it this morning.

Jeri leans against the woodshed, smiling as a few wisps of snowflakes kiss her cheeks. "You ought to know I switched sides in this battle of yours."

"What battle?" I swing the axe.

Jeri waits until the log splits before she speaks. "The one with you and Miss Sloan Hanson," she says in a breathy whisper as she flutters her lashes. "She won me over, and I'm on her side."

"What side? She's the crazy woman who wanted to drive through an avalanche. I think I'm more of a hero."

She snorts. "Crazy woman, huh? Never heard you insult a guest. She must really get to you."

Get to me is an understatement. I hardly know what I'm doing. I wish Sloan would leave and take this smoldering turmoil boiling under my skin, a feeling like I'm about to split at the seams. But that same feeling has me hoping she'll stay. At least long enough I can wade through this haze in my brain. I'm angry at Sloan, but not for anything she did. No, I'm angry she *listened* to me. She professed how much we mattered, then me, the idiot, told her to bury it. Told her to forget me.

The hurt of it all multiplied when I reached out to Sloan after Abigail came to me and I was left wanting. Sloan took to heart what a confused seventeen-year-old kid said once. And that is my twisted way of justifying why I'm a combustible ball of fury around this woman. Yet at the same time I want to wrap her in my arms and revive the only relationship outside of family that has ever mattered.

"Earth to Rowan," Jeri says waving her hand in front of my face. "Where did you go?"

I shake my head and gather a few of the logs. "I'm fine. Is Abs ready?"

"Yes," Jeri says. "But all joking aside, are you okay? I've never seen you this distracted before."

"Jer, it's . . . complicated."

"I'm pretty smart, and think I could keep up." She opens the door for me and we both stomp our shoes on the mat before heading to the fireplace in the living room. She waits patiently while I stack the logs and start the fire.

When the smoke settles and the flames take shape, I sit back on my heels and glance at her. “Have you ever had a friend who knows more about you than your own family?”

Jeri considers the question then nods. “Yeah, she’s my cousin though. We’re sort of like sisters.”

“Same idea,” I tell her as I poke the wood. “That was me and Sloan.”

“Well why are you being so rude to her then?”

“I’m not being . . .” I groan. “I wasn’t being rude. I was trying to keep her stubborn butt from flying off the highway into a snowbank.”

“Rowan come on. You’ve been prickly. Why?”

I don’t want to explain it, so I wave the idea away and say, “We just lost touch.”

“I think it’s more than that.”

I scrub my face, letting the words come. Maybe it’s time they’re said. “I hurt her eight years ago, okay. She moved away, we lost touch, then I became the party soldier who drowned himself in booze and a good time. I was someone she would’ve been disgusted with.”

“Harsh,” Jeri says. “You didn’t give her a chance to prove herself.”

“Yeah, I know,” I say briskly. “By the time I got myself together, I don’t know, it had been too long.”

Jeri opens her mouth to say something, but we're interrupted when Abigail crashes into the room. "I lost another tooth!" She stands, spread-legged in the doorway, one arm holding the prize over her head as though it's a trophy.

"What?" I say, forcing a grin. "We're going to be feeding you pudding all day if you keep dropping those things."

She giggles and comes to show us. When Abigail came to live with me, out of all the gross things kids do, I hadn't anticipated teeth dangling from gums being the thing that made me gag. I hate wiggly teeth. And now she's losing some of her molars, those are worse.

"Ready for pizza, squirt?" I ask messing up her hair.

She nods vigorously. "I'm starving."

"Hungry," Jeri corrects. "You're hungry. Starving would imply I don't waste away feeding you people every day."

Abigail doesn't get it and skips to the kitchen where Jeri already has the dough and toppings laid out, but my gut sinks to my shoes. Sitting on the long bench at the farmhouse table Sloan is spreading red sauce over one of the pizzas.

Her curls are pulled up in a ponytail and she's in a T-shirt now and a pair of leggings. She looks up when we come inside, and I must've forgotten how captivating those eyes are. With a single look, I'm undone.

I strip off my coat and force myself to look away.

Sloan isn't the only guest invited to our ritual pizza night. The newlyweds are there too, and per stereotype they made a heart shaped pizza.

"Figured we better feed these good people since everything is still a ghost town," Jeri explains.

"There's supposed to be another storm, so I doubt it'll be opened much tomorrow," says the new Mrs. Prentis.

Sloan's shoulders slump. "Really?"

Prentis grins with a nod. "I didn't think I'd love a honeymoon in the middle of winter, but I" – a kiss to her husband – "am" – *kiss* – "loving it."

I hide a laugh when Abigail pretends to gag.

"I bet you are," Sloan says softly.

My lips twitch, but I stop the smile trying to break through. Maybe Jeri is right, and I am being prickly around Sloan. It's not as though I want this big, awkward bulge between us, but how is this supposed to go? We brush our last face to face conversation under the rug? Am I supposed to pretend like I didn't try to make amends, try to get my best friend back three years ago? Then there is the trouble about me not being capable of talking around Sloan because she's not the girl with braces, and silver eyeliner that she insisted would be the next hot makeup trend. She's a woman; successful, burdened, beautiful. A cruel reminder of what I let slip through my fingers. Sloan brings a heady sort of feeling that leaves me wanting to put my head between my knees and breathe deeply like I tell Abigail to do.

I am about to sit at the opposite end of the table when Abigail marches her pizza dough and pan and nestles right next to Sloan. My niece looks to me then pats the seat on the bench next to her. She's found our spot. Jeri is already holding out a pan with unbaked dough and bowls of toppings for me to mess with. I glare at her when she winks at me.

This isn't some romantic movie. It's real. We're real people who have a past. And not exactly one with a pleasant ending.

Licking my lips, I settle next to Abigail.

Sloan flashes a glance at me, then turns back to arranging her pepperoni and . . . yes, pineapple. I'm not the only one who notices.

"Yuck," Abigail says. "Uncle Ro likes that stuff too."

Sloan grins. "I know."

My palms feel sweaty.

"Gross," Abigail says, nose wrinkled. "That's weird."

"Sloan is weird, she's the one who forced me to like pineapple on pizza, Abs," I say before I can stop myself.

Sloan's smile fades when she peeks over the top of Abigail's head and meets my eyes. I clear my throat and focus on my low-pineapple pizza. She does use more than me.

"Are you friends?" Abigail asks.

Sloan keeps her smile, but the corner of her lips twitch. She doesn't look at me. "We were."

"So you knew my mom!" That smile comes, the one Abigail wears whenever we tell her stories about Jenny.

A shadow passes over Sloan's face, the briefest one, before she grins. "I did know your mom. Oh, man I was so jealous of Jenny when I was a kid."

"Really!" Abigail plops a clump of shredded cheese in the center of her pizza, straddles the bench, and waits intently for more. "Why?"

Sloan doesn't hesitate. "Because Jenny was like a princess to me. Long, brown hair, bright eyes. She was beautiful, but not just outside; she was the nicest girl. Everyone loved Jenny. Even though I was younger, she still invited me to movies sometimes." Sloan smirks at Abigail who is beaming. "You know, you remind me of your mom. So much. All the good things about Jenny, I think you got them, kid."

A sting aches in the back of my throat, as though someone hit me there. Abigail radiates, she sits a little straighter, worries a little less. When I get up the nerve, I flick my eyes to Sloan and mouth *Thank you.*

She doesn't say anything simply turns back to her pineapple-soaked pizza.

The Prentises didn't last long with us and left the moment their pizzas were devoured. Jeri handles the dining room cleanup while Abigail, me, and Sloan take to the kitchen.

I'm smiling. I know, it's weird.

Somewhere during the pizza night, Abigail finally yanked free a few pieces of the past. Sloan told her about moving to Silver Creek, and how the first kid to talk to her was some skinny boy on the playground.

"He told me he was the king of the slides," she whispered.

"I did not," I said.

"He did. But I moved here from New York. Do you think I let some punk kid tell me what's what?"

Abigail snorted a squeaky laugh and shook her head.

"Dang straight I didn't. I climbed up that slide, the wrong way, of course, yanked on his ankle where he was standing all rough and tough, ripped his feet out from under him, and took him all the way down with me. After that, he just wouldn't leave me alone and followed me like a little, lost puppy."

Jeri had barked a laugh and Abigail repeatedly mocked that I'd been beaten by a girl.

"Well," I said, as I gathered plates. "Sloan doesn't tell the story right. I went down so the bigger kids wouldn't pick on her. They were coming, she just didn't see them."

Now, at the sink I don't feel as if I'm drowning. At least not all the time. Sometimes she'll come close when she hands me a stack of plates or cups and I'll smell the citrus of her shampoo, or the vanilla of her perfume.

When those moments come, I bite the inside of my cheek. To keep grounded, and all.

She hands me the plate Jeri used to hold the Canadian bacon. Our fingers brush. She draws in a sharp breath, and I understand the feeling. For a moment I freeze.

Until the sound of breaking glass interrupts.

Sloan jolts and I whip around. Abigail is standing over the pile of glass, a plate in her hand, one drinking glass tipped on its side, and another smashed at her feet. She's trembling and I can see the swell of tears forming before she probably even notices the storm has arrived.

"I-I-I'm sorry," Abigail whimpers. Tears come in big, terrified drops on her cheeks. "I didn't mean to—"

"Abs, it's good," I hurry to say. She's breaking down and Sloan doesn't need to be here. Abigail doesn't need to see someone gawk at her, maybe think negatively about her behavior. The very idea of it makes my skin flush in heat.

Abigail starts to sob. "I didn't mean to." She gulps three deep breaths. "I just . . . I just wanted to help. I'm sorry."

I start to lose count how many times she says sorry before I'm at her side. I guess when I go into *Help Abigail Mode,* I tune out because I never noticed Sloan beat me to my niece.

"Hey," she says, her arms around Abigail. It looks like Sloan is squeezing her, almost kneading her shoulders like dough. But it gets Abigail to stop shuddering. "Can you take a deep breath in through your nose?" Sloan whispers. "Good, like that. Now blow it out your mouth like you're going to blow out a candle. Good. Here I'll do it with you a few times."

I'm stunned. A little awed and bewildered at the same time. Abigail's teary eyes stay with Sloan as they do: one breath in, one long breath out. I don't know how, but it's helping. Abigail wipes her sleeve under her nose, then wipes her snotty sleeve over her eyes.

"I'm sorry," she says.

Sloan smiles. "It was an accident, and accidents happen."

Jeri comes into the kitchen. "Whoopsie. I'll grab the broom. Abs, why don't you come help me, but careful where you step."

Abigail glances to me and I smile. "We clean up after ourselves, right kid?"

She nods and her eyes are glistening. With her head down she follows Jeri. The kitchen is silent for too long. Time is fickle when quiet grows tense. What feels like two hours, likely is a few seconds.

"Thanks," I say softly. "For whatever you did there."

Sloan wheels on me, lips tight. "She has massive anxiety, Rowan."

My brow furrows. "Yeah, I know, what—"

"You need to watch what is said to her. Does she normally get in trouble for breaking a stupid glass?"

Whoa. Sloan is . . . wait. She's mad at *me*? My jaw tightens as I stomp closer. "I do everything I can to make sure Abigail feels safe, and loved, and wanted. Don't lecture me when you have no idea what goes on here."

"I didn't know, but I just got a front row seat."

"Yeah, to a truckload of assumptions." I drag my fingers through my hair. "Thanks for the help Sloan, but I think I know Abigail a little better than you."

She gathers her bag that is sitting by the kitchen doorway, mouth tight. "I might not know Abigail, but I know exactly what she's feeling when that happens. Trust me, that sort of anxiety, it comes from the environment around a kid."

And at that she storms out of the kitchen, leaving me trying to keep up to the swift change in the room.

"She sure told you," Jeri says with irony at my back. Thankfully, Abigail is not with her.

I shake my head. "She just doesn't know the story."

"Yeah, clearly." Jeri slips next to me and leverages onto the edge of the table until her legs dangle off the side. "Rowan, I know how you feel about my life advice."

"You don't care."

She chuckles. "Nope, I'm going to give it anyway. I don't think it would be the worst thing if you clued her in."

"Why? Let her think what she wants. She'll be gone in a couple nights."

Jeri shrugs and swipes her curly hair off one shoulder. "True. Blue skies should be here by Friday. I'm saying it because of the way your face lit up tonight. Deny it all you want, but there is a big part of that black heart of yours that likes having Sloan around again."

"Leave my black heart alone."

Jeri smiles and claps me on the shoulder. "Whatever kid. What do I know? I'm just older, wiser, more experienced."

"You aren't even five years older, my friend."

"Still wiser. Listen, Abigail took to her, she just told me how Sloan calmed her down. Pretty cool if you ask me."

I pause and stare at the empty doorway where Sloan stormed away. She knows exactly what Abigail feels? What did that mean? Did she feel this way when we were kids? Her homelife was wild sometimes, but we usually just hung out when it was bad, or we'd go to the library, or watch stars from my trampoline. Did she break down like Abigail and I didn't know?

"Ah, I like when you're thinking about what I say," Jeri says as she hops off the table and takes her coat out of the closet in the back of the kitchen. "Well, keep giving it some thought. I'll see you tomorrow."

Jeri lives in the guest house out back during the week or when it's snowy like tonight and watching her go, I think I ought to just offer her the place. She runs the inn as much as me and should know I recognize it.

Her words matter too. This is a chance I didn't take eight years ago. To clear the air between me and Sloan now that yet another misunderstanding has creeped up.

Tomorrow. I swallow hard. We'll talk tomorrow.

Maybe it doesn't matter.

Then again, maybe it does.

Chapter 5

Sloan

According to the Department of Transportation—I'm here for at least another night. I groan and flop back onto the bed. It's not even six in the morning, and already my stomach is in knots, my chest heavy. How am I supposed to open the Moosehead Lodge if I can't even get there?

It's fine. No one can control the weather. Not even Mark Bridger.

Another ten times of repeating that and the tightness in my chest eases slightly, enough I get out of bed and take to a few yoga stretches. I'm a creature of habit now, and missed my sunrise routine yesterday. I noticed.

When I shower and am halfway put together, I consider curling back into bed and reading, or something frivolous, but decide I can handle a few items on the to-do list virtually. I shoot a text to Moreen, the hospitality manager and arrange a video meeting for this afternoon. She returns with a lengthy response, telling me in one single text about the work she still needs to accomplish, but is completely stressed because of the road closures.

All that leads into her ex-husband's terrible driving habits in the snow which has given her a complex about ice and tires.

She makes me smile. The lodge has a good team and I want their hard work to shine on Christmas Eve. Not for Mark Bridger, not for Luke, not for me. They've earned the recognition.

I pull out my laptop and start arranging the room to look semi-professional, then groan. My power cord is missing. Of course, I hadn't expected to be trapped here for days. Still, my three-thirds battery life on my computer won't survive the video calls I have planned. With any luck I'll be able to sneak into town and head over to Jones Market. The hodge-podge store usually carries a random supply of electronics, often tucked in the same aisle as toilet paper because that makes sense.

My stomach grumbles and I'm reminded of Jeri's cinnamon rolls. She wasn't wrong. I ate the one she made yesterday, and I think I might stay forever if she keeps shoving those down my throat. But there is the problem that Rowan Graham lives here.

A little grunt of disgust bubbles into my throat. Rowan isn't Abigail's biological father, no, but from what I can see he's her only parent, and clearly he's inadequately praising that kid. She was terrified of punishment, I saw the look, *had* that look a thousand times in my own eyes. From experience that sort of fear comes from words spoken in the past. Rowan better watch what he says to her. He's all broody, and I know he was in the army. Maybe his years as a soldier made him strict and high strung. But this isn't an Army barracks. This is a kid who needs a soft place to fall.

I shake my head, wondering what happened with Abigail's dad. I didn't know Jenny's husband well, but I'm not sure he knew how to be a husband well either. Sort of like he is as a dad it seems.

My phone buzzes on the nightstand. Ugh, speaking of inadequate parents. I answer because if I don't, then I'll get ten more calls. "Hi, Tracy."

"Sloan, you're awake."

"So are you." My voice is flat.

"Well, I am an early riser."

My father's wife speaks through her nose, and I am prone to drift to other thoughts whenever we speak, uninterested in whatever my stepmother says most days. "What can I do for you?"

Tracy snorts. "So formal, lighten up. Ever since Luke ended things, you've been one big, ball of gloom. Not that I blame you, mmmm, he is such a sexy man. I'd be sad if he left too."

"Don't you think it's weird that my father's wife is going on about how hot my ex-boyfriend is? And second, if you want Luke, take him. If you recall he's not exactly the faithful type."

"My gosh," Tracy huffs. "I was teasing."

"Tracy, I'm about to start work," I lie because really I just want cinnamon rolls. "What do you need?"

"I brought up Luke for a reason," she says. "He called your dad the other day—"

My stomach sinks.

"And told us to call you for a room at your lodge. A suite, so we have plenty of room to get dressed for the party on Christmas Eve. I wanted to speak with you about getting together for the holidays. I know you like to do your own thing, or go to Kristine's—"

"My mother's house," I say with a bite.

"Whatever," Tracy mutters. "Look, I know your dad would really like to spend a little bit of time with you, and to be honest, I don't think he minded that Luke called. Maybe you should try to work things out. Your dad likes him."

My dad knows nothing about how good relationships should be, not his own and not mine. That's what I want to say. It's what I should say.

"So," she goes on when I keep quiet. "Can we expect a warm welcome, or this frosty ice queen persona you've taken on lately?"

"Does it really matter?" I ask in earnest. "It's not like Dad and me are close. At all."

"And who's to blame for that? Shane has tried. You won't let him get close to you."

"Thanks for the father-daughter advice, Tracy, but really I'm good with where we stand. He made that amply clear over the years."

"Oh, yes. Poor you, you had a dad who pushed you."

Is that what she'd call it? I close my eyes and practice what I preach. Deep breath in through my nose, one deep breath out.

"He wanted you to succeed, and from what Mr. Bridger has been saying, you are. Thanks to your dad."

I think I had something to do with it.

"Caring about someone isn't always hugs and 'atta girls'," Tracy goes on. "Oh, and Bridger told him about the position you were offered in Alpine."

"What, I—"

"So, instead of resenting the man that dragged out your potential, you kicking and screaming the entire way, maybe show a bit of gratitude. Especially since we'll be neighbors. You wouldn't want to set such an awful example for Tiny would you?"

I hold my breath. My little sister, the adorable tween offspring of my father and Tracy. Tiny Hallie is the only reason I plaster a fake smile on my face around them. She's a gem, and the one good thing that came out of that union.

"Will you bring her up?"

"Depends on you." Tracy's a wretched manipulator. How she has raised such a sweetheart in Hallie, I'll never—oh, yes I do know—because Hallie spends more time with Gretchen, her nanny, than our dad and Tracy. My stepmother smacks her lips on the other side. "Sloan, your father holds more stake in this than you, and you need to respect that position."

True, Shane Hanson is on the board of directors for the new resort. When we were together, Luke schmoozed my dad into dropping some of his seven-figure salary into the project. But my dad knows snow and is on the board of directors of two Utah ski resorts. He was an obvious choice. Again, I wonder if that is another reason I have my job. No, I earned this through merit. I must believe that.

"When will you be here?" I whisper.

"The night before Christmas Eve. Can you arrange for a room at the lodge?"

My head feels a little heavy. "Uh, I'll try. The roads are closed, so I haven't been there, and there is a bit of a plumbing issue, so—"

"Aren't you in charge?"

"Yes."

She sighs loudly. "We were under the impression it was going to be spectacular. I hope you know your father's reputation is on the line too."

What she's really saying is: You, evil stepdaughter, better not embarrass us. "I'll make sure there's a room. For all the guests. Everyone matters at the lodge."

"That's sweet," Tracy says arrogantly. "Then I'll plan to see you next week."

We end with awkward, resentful goodbyes. I feel for Hallie. She is only twelve and must live under their roof for at least six more years. I was forced for only eighteen months before I went to college. What a time that was. All at once my dad insisted I would be better suited at the private school above greater Salt Lake City. My mom was traveling for her marketing job, trying to hold our small, broken family together, and in the end agreed. She'd hoped it would give me more stability.

All it really did was tear me away from my home and friends. I wince. Those friends like Rowan. Never mind that was the same year that Jenny died, and I broke my last good relationship by telling Rowan I loved him.

I bite the tip of my tongue. Being here is bringing it all back in a rush. I would like nothing more than to run away to a cabin off the grid where no one will ever find me again. But I can't do that, I won't.

I lift my chin and finish getting ready, smooth out the bed and make my way downstairs. At the front of the inn I pause to inspect the damage from any storm through the night. The parking lot is packed in fresh powder, but it's not snowing now. I can see new tracks from an ATV and expect Rowan is likely out plowing his way around the inn.

"Goooood Morning," Jeri sings as she rounds the corner. "You're the VIP guest this morning since the others checked out."

My eyes widen. "Wait, the roads, are they—"

"Sorry," she says hurriedly. "They left and went back into town where roads are wide open. Your direction—" Jeri shakes her head. "Sorry, girlfriend. Still avalanched as ever."

I rub the bridge of my nose.

"But," Jeri says. "The good news is when you're the one and only guest, you get to pick the menu for breakfast. So, tomorrow what'll it be? I make a mean French toast casserole, or granola stuffed baked apples, or a vegetable quiche. Take your pick and let me know by noon."

I offer her a quick grin and turn at the sound of clumping steps on the staircase. Abigail comes downstairs, lips pouting, and a backpack slung over her shoulders.

"Why the long face?" I ask.

"I gotta go to school," she says with a dramatic sigh as she sits on the window seat, staring longingly at the new snow drifts.

"Oh, it's not so bad," Jeri says. "The snow will be here when you get back."

"S'not the same." Abigail leans her elbows on the sill of the window and sighs again.

Jeri winks at me and crosses out breakfast casserole on the chalkboard menu next to the dining room. "Sorry, the Prentises had three servings each this morning."

"I'm more in a sweet roll and tea mood anyway."

"That I can do for you."

"Hey, you said the roads were open into town, right?"

"They are," she says.

"Good. I need a power cord and thought I'd drive in this morning. Plus, my little travel-sized toothpaste is on its last squirt." I stare at my snow-covered rental car. "Not looking forward to scraping the windows on that thing though."

"You can ride with us."

The low rumble of Rowan's voice shoots a wash of sensation down to my toes. He slips off a pair of snowy gloves and wipes his boots on the heavy-duty mat by the back door behind the desk.

"Yeah!" Abigail says. "The bus won't come up here when it's still so snowy, so Uncle Ro drives me to school. Come!"

"Oh," I say, avoiding Rowan's eyes. "No, I have a car. I can drive myself."

"The truck is already warm," Rowan says. "I have to stop at Jones' anyway."

Why is he pushing this? Jeri is nodding, even if she's not looking at us and Abigail is beaming that grin with gaps from missing teeth. I choose to smile at the little girl. "Okay, I'll hitch a ride." Then I look back at Rowan and add a touch of caution to my voice. "If that's alright."

"Said it was," he tells me as he hands Abigail her coat. "Come on squirt. We're going to be late."

Chapter 6
Sloan

"Have your book?" Rowan asks Abigail, his eyes on the rearview mirror, watching her gather her things in the back seat of the truck.

"Got it," she says, waving a chapter book with a cartoon dog on the front.

"Okay, see you after school. Love you, kid."

"Love you!" she says. "Bye Sloan."

"Bye," I add.

She bursts out of the backseat and is greeted by a school drop off attendant before following the swarm of elementary students carefully walking along the icy sidewalks into the building. I grin. Everything is so similar. The brown brick and statue of a lynx next to the flagpole. The same pine trees line the edges of the school, and like when I went here, teachers are bundled up like they've spent the night in an igloo as they shovel and salt the walks, high-fiving kids as they go.

Rowan drives us out of the parent loop, saying nothing. But I suppose there isn't much to say. I was irritated with him last night, then he invited me to drive with him. I thought maybe he'd say something about last night, but he's said nothing to me, only Abigail. Now we're alone and it seems we'll be much the same.

I swallow, hating the silence more than the potential argument. "Looks the same."

"What?"

I point my thumb at the school behind us. "Still looks the same."

Half his mouth curls into a grin. "Yeah. Miss Hollander is still there."

"No way. She was a dinosaur when we were kids."

"Still there, cracking that stupid yard stick against the board."

His grin widens and a warmth spreads in the bottom of my stomach. I forgot Rowan had a dimple on his right cheek. Even with the dark scruff on his face I can see it and remember how I loved it back then, but was too afraid to admit it. Lacy Stevens wasn't, nor Holly Smith, or Eva Harper. Once we'd hit high school more than one girl noticed Rowan's changing physique. Though, even with his ruggedness taking shape, I hadn't expected him to transform into a guy all muscle and tone. Thinking of his old flames leads me to wonder what sort of women Rowan keeps now. Jeri seems more friendly with him than anything. Maybe someone in town has his interest. Then I wonder why I care at all. It's not my business.

We're quiet until we reach Jones Market, not a long silence since the store is only a mile down the road, but enough to bring the awkward tension back. Rowan walks at my side into the store, his hands shoved inside his coat pockets. If I'm stuck at the Holly Berry Inn much longer, then I'll need to clear this air between us. Maybe we ought to clear everything, as in going back to when it fell apart.

Perhaps he drives me crazy now, maybe he is too strict with his niece, but as much as I fight it, Rowan Graham still matters. I hate that we are strangers to each other.

"I'll be in the toys," he tells me in his husky rasp.

I lift a brow, but don't ask and head toward the electronics vs. toilet paper aisle. It takes a whole two minutes before I'm singing praises to little Jones Market for having a power cord. I slip over to the toiletries and grab some more toothpaste and a new lip balm because I have a squirrely habit of collecting them. I figure Rowan will be at the front of the store, but the only customers are a woman with four different types of jelly and a gentleman with a cart filled with a broom, mop, at least six plastic garbage cans.

I dance around the aisles heading to the toys where I find him holding two pink boxes with different Barbie dolls inside.

"Looks like you have a fun night planned," I say, giving up and allowing the grin to come.

He lifts his gaze, and a bit of red tints his cheeks. "Abby has a birthday party on Friday." He holds up the dolls. "Which one?"

I tap my chin and abandon the Barbies and move toward a section filled with do-it-yourself jewelry. "From what I've seen of Abigail she doesn't seem the type to play with dolls."

"Aren't these like a default girl toy?"

I snort. "I never played with Barbies that much."

"Because you hung out with me."

My breath catches in my throat. The way he turns away, I'm not sure he meant to bring up our lengthy history.

"True," I say, voice rough. "But you also pouted if you didn't get your way. I guess I didn't see the point in arguing by bringing Barbies into the mix."

Rowan's mouth opens. "I did not, but I don't think dolls in skimpy little dresses were cooler than being outside."

"I'll have you know Barbie is a doctor *and* an astronaut." I snatch the boxes out of his hands and replace them with a big jewelry making kit. "If Abigail's friends are like her, I'd guess they would have more fun with something like this."

Rowan smiles shyly as he inspects the box. "They are kind of creative, I guess. Thanks."

"Sure." Time to return to our short, terse way of speaking.

We pay for our respective items and drift back into the cold. Sounds of Christmas are everywhere. Most shops play *Winter Wonderland* on their speakers, or *Joy to the World*. On the corner a cheery bell from a Salvation Army Santa rings donations into his little, red pail. The endless evergreens are all decked in lights, and in the daylight the gleam of the gold and silver ornaments decorating the city building trees sends a glare across the sidewalk.

Rowan starts his truck and rubs his hands together as he adjusts the power of the heater. I shiver, my jaw clenched, waiting for the temperature to rise. We weren't gone for that long, but frigid cold always hangs over Silver Creek after a storm.

"Hey," Rowan says softly. His knuckles go white as he tightens his grip on the steering wheel. "I don't know what you have planned, but would you want to grab something to eat before we head back?"

The expression I intend to offer is one of surprise, but the way he looks aghast I safely assume I'm either glaring at him or grimacing.

"I just . . ." He pauses. "I'd like to explain some stuff about last night."

Last night. About how I basically yelled at him and accused him of being a sorry excuse for a caregiver. Right. Sounds epically fun. I still say, "Oh, okay. Sure."

He offers a brisk nod and begins to pull out of the parking lot.

"Wait," I say. "I do need to be back by one thirty. I have a video call with an employee."

He glances at the clock. It's only nine twenty. "Plenty of time."

Okay then. I'm not sure I release the breath I keep pent up until we drive three blocks to the old diner on the corner of Main and Blossom Street. Right in what locals call 'the hub' of downtown Silver Creek. The idea of it draws a small grin out of me. At population twelve hundred, this is hardly a downtown hub.

"Just as I left it," I say when we head inside. Regulars in their tattered baseball caps sip black coffee and talk political things. Waitresses in pink, collared dresses and white aprons refill waters and mugs, a few Silver Creek police officers shovel pancakes and bacon in before they're called back to the beat.

"Rowan, good to see you hon. Sit anywhere." A waitress with silvery blue hair and a beaded lanyard on her glasses says with a wink.

"Thanks Shelly," he says.

"Shelly Patts?" I whisper, squinting as though it'll help me see better. "As in the woman who called Sheriff Bloomer on us for picking her roses?"

Rowan chuckles and slides into a booth near the back. "That's her. Started working here after her husband retired. According to her, this job saves her marriage and without it she'd start to hate the sight of the man."

I laugh softly and strip back my coat at the same time Shelly bounces over to our table.

"How you doin' sweetie?" she asks Rowan. "Business good? How's your parents?"

"Good, Shell," he says. "We're doing fine."

She flashes her dark eyes to me and grins at first, then her pink lips drop. "Criminy, uh, uh, Hanson. Sloanie Hanson is that you?"

My pulse picks up a notch. I didn't think, well, more hoped no one would recognize me. "Yeah. How are you Ms. Patts?"

"Listen to her," Shelly says. "Girl, has living large in cities gotten to your manners? You can call me Shelly. Good heavens, I was just chatting with your mom around Halloween. She makes the sweetest cakes, doesn't she? How is she liking Boulder?"

My brow furrows. I talk to my mom at least once a week and don't recall a single time she's mentioned that she keeps in touch with anyone from Silver Creek. "Uh, yeah she likes making cakes now, and she enjoys Boulder, I think. Misses the small town feel up here, I'm sure."

"Well, who doesn't?" Shelly says. "You hooligans caused quite a stir up here yourselves. My roses thank you for maturing."

Now Rowan joins me in laughing. Shelly insists I try the chef's new favorite, a new spin on an egg muffin, apparently. I order a cup of herbal tea, a water, and Rowan does the same except takes a Belgian waffle. When we're alone with our drinks, I stare out the window to ignore how my pulse hammers in my ears.

Rowan fiddles with the sugar packets. I close my eyes and take a deep breath. This is silly, us not being able to talk. There were nights my mom would barge into my room, well after one in the morning, and catch me under my sheets talking on the phone to this man. We were most often plotting our great pranks we constantly pulled at school, or talking about boys I liked, girls he liked. Anything, but not now.

I tap the table to get his attention. "Alright, set me straight."

His brow wrinkles. "What?"

"You wanted to talk about last night, I can only assume it's to set me straight."

"Oh." He adjusts on the bench. "Yeah, actually, it is."

I open my hands. "Well . . ."

"I, uh, I wanted to give a little background on Abigail, that's all. What you saw last night, it's a thing. She hasn't had it easy since Jenny died."

"I imagine not," I say softly.

"Anyway, she has this crippling need to please, and if she feels like she's failing, well, you saw what happened. Before my parents moved, we started her in counseling, and it helped. She hasn't gone for about six months because I'm supposed to try and implement everything at home."

My chest hurts. Regret is like a dull knife. I shouldn't have jumped down his throat last night and I have a feeling I'm about to learn exactly why I was not in the right.

"Listen Sloan," he goes on. "I'm not perfect with Abigail, never pretended to be, but one thing I've never done is tell that girl she's not enough. Since she's been mine full-time the last three years, I've been trying everything I know how to undo that *poisonous* thought in her head. She deserves more than I can give, I'm sure."

I lace my fingers together to keep from taking his and stare at the table. "May I ask . . . what happened to her dad?"

Shelly arrives with our food then, and tops off our waters. Turns out the spin on the muffin is simply a sausage patty and a few pieces of bacon on top of the egg. Rowan doesn't eat for a long moment, his eyes zero in on my toppling breakfast sandwich.

"Her dad," I press. "Where is he?"

Rowan draws in a sharp breath. "Scott didn't handle being a single dad very well. When Abby was four he asked for a sort of joint custody arrangement with my parents. But my dad was struggling then, I don't know if you know but he has chronic Bronchitis that just kept getting worse. So I came home to help."

"That's when you left the Army?"

"Seemed better than reenlisting," he admits. "Scott filtered in and out, but soon every other weekend started turning into one weekend a month, to every other month. It was really hard on my parents. You know they had Jen and me later in life and with my dad's health declining, it was tough. Scott wasn't a good husband to begin with, remember?"

I nod, vividly remembering nights Rowan would vent about his new brother-in-law as we threw rocks in the creek.

"I guess when Jen got pregnant, he was worse. Blamed her for making his life harder. He was in this hot-shot graduate program or whatever back then, and Abigail was a wrench in the plans."

Remembering this part of the past hurts. Jenny was four years older than us, but I didn't lie to Abigail. She was a beautiful human in every way. She'd married right out of high school. I still remember her dress, and thinking she looked like a queen. She was pregnant by the time she turned twenty, and in a way it was a blessing. Without Abigail they'd have never found the tumor. According to Rowan back then, the doctors said finding it was able to give her a few extra months to say goodbye. Dying at twenty-one isn't right.

"He wasn't good to Abigail?" I ask after a pause.

Rowan shakes his head. "I'll give him a little credit, he tried. At first. He gave her a house, a room, food. But he used her. To get women, sympathy, a leg up in his job. As Abigail got older that's when we started noticing how nervous she was about everything. I remember once she forgot to brush her teeth before bed. When my mom asked her, Abigail ran and hid in the closet. She just sobbed, so sure we'd be angry with her."

I cover my mouth, my stomach sick.

"But it wasn't just the crying," he says. "It's the things she said. She was positive we wouldn't let her stay at our house, or we'd send her away somewhere if she ever stepped out of line."

"Was he telling her he'd give her up?" I ask, deliriously angry all at once.

"I asked Abs why she thought we'd get rid of her, and she told me because her mom left. I explained that Jen died, and if she could've, she would've stayed with her every second of the day. But Abigail said her dad would sometimes tell her if she didn't behave, or if she embarrassed him, then he might decide he didn't want to stay with her too."

"Rowan," I say in a sort of gasp.

"Anyway," he says, leaning back in the booth and picking at a few bits of waffle. "When she was six, Scott got a job in Connecticut and asked my parents to take temporary guardianship while he got settled. Well, that's when my dad went downhill. I took the guardianship so my mom could manage everything with Dad, and here we are three years later. I'm getting ready to move for permanent guardianship at the new year."

"Does he even call her?"

Rowan nods. "Like once a month. He visits sometimes too, but it's been about seven months since they saw each other last."

I stare at my hands. "I'm sorry." It isn't hard to say.

"I wasn't mad at what you said, I just wanted to explain."

"I'm still sorry. I shouldn't have assumed you would be so hard on her."

Rowan takes a bite and stares out the window at the passersby on the street. We eat for a few minutes, saying nothing. He's moody, to be sure, but Rowan is still the most loyal soul I've ever met. He's been her guardian for three years, and I rack my brain trying to think of any other twenty-two-year-old guy who'd step in and be a dad to their niece.

"Is that why you bought the inn?" I ask after a moment. "When you got Abigail."

He turns his eyes to me. "Yeah. Bart needed an out, and I liked the idea of being able to make a living but be available to her. My job at the time was just as busy as Scott, and when my parents had to move, I didn't want her to have that chaos again."

I slouch in my bench, and cross my arms over my chest. "I wish you were a jerk."

He coughs through a drink in his water. "What?"'

A smile teases my lips. "If you were a jerk, I wouldn't feel so stupid about my overreaction."

"Ah," he says, even breaking a grin of his own. "So selfish reasons."

"Always."

Rowan leans forward onto his elbows, voice low. "I'm not a jerk to Abigail, but that doesn't mean I haven't been one . . . to others."

I swallow with effort and take a forceful sip of water. Those eyes are breaking into me like weak glass. His meaning is obvious, and I don't know what to say, so I start to eat quietly because I'm a coward. Simple as that.

"By the way," he says when I've finished half the greasy sandwich. "What did you do with Abs? It's like you just jumped in and she calmed down. Normally she would be crying for an hour over a broken glass."

Ugh. This is an awkward topic too, but I do my best to keep it light. "Come on, Rowan," I say. "You remember my dad. If I got an 'A' it was a grunt of approval, and a threat that I'd better keep it that way or else. I get the need to please, that's all."

He watches me, a bit of puzzlement in the smooth brown of his eyes. "Nope," he says, breaking his scrutiny. "I never saw you freak out like that."

I shake my head. "Because I never did in front of people."

He frowns. "I don't like that. I don't like knowing you kept something awful like that to yourself and handled it alone."

My heart hammers in my chest, but I hide it with a tilt to my head. "What would you have done as a kid? Told my dad to shut his mouth?"

"For you? In a second." Then he clears his throat and tacks on, "Back then."

Right. Back then, not now. Because we're not friends anymore. We're acquaintances. Acquaintances. I scoff and finish off my tea. We're not acquaintances, I am simply too discomposed at the idea of breaking into that box of feelings I don't want to face again.

"Well, if it's any consolation," I say with a touch of mirth. "Girls with an anxious complex sometimes grow up knowing how to breathe and calm really nicely."

"Yeah," he says, a shy grin on his face. "So, I can expect Abigail to be a Yogi who drinks tea and sniffs essential oils?"

"You know, it's sort of creepy how well you've described me." I laugh. So does Rowan. "I'm not so bad, I guess."

"No," he says slowly. "You're not so bad."

I tug on the ends of my curls to hide the flush in my face. "Besides, Abby has you. She'll be better than me. A Yogi with the tea, but maybe not huffing essential oils."

That makes him laugh again as we get up to pay our bill. He reaches into his wallet and I reach for mine, but his fingers brush the back of my elbow. "No," he says. "Let me."

"It's fine Rowan," I say, ignoring the way the skin on the back of my arm is still warm.

"Please," he insists. "Call it a peace offering for being so, what did Jeri call me? — prickly, since you came."

I snort. "I like Jeri, and she's spot on. You are prickly. Like a cactus."

"Those are the coolest plants just so you know."

I slug his shoulder, transported back in time for half a breath, and lead the way out the door. We aren't as quiet on the way home, not like the drive into town. We talk about nothing important, a lot about cacti, and some about Rowan's apparent aversion to Abigail's missing teeth.

I feel a bit lighter when we step back into the front lobby. Rowan gives me a shy kind of smile then sets to his endless workload keeping the ancient building from crumbling on us all, and I reluctantly go upstairs to prepare for my video calls.

But for the first time in a long time, the smile on my face, it's real.

Chapter 7

Rowan

"Is Sloan your best friend?"

I pause, halfway to returning our latest edition of *Captain Underpants* back on the bookshelf. "What? Who told you that?"

Abigail nestles deeper into her blankets, hugging the purple bunny my mom gave her two Christmases ago. "Nana," she says. "She told me you guys used to be more than friends, you were *best* friends."

I return the book then sit on the foot of her bed. "Yeah, we used to be best friends."

"How come she never comes over then?"

"Well," I say with a sigh. "Sometimes grownups move away from their friends." Then I think better of that because Abigail will stress over the idea of leaving Kat, her best friend, so I change directions. "And sometimes friends like me, hurt friends like her. I wasn't nice to Sloan once, Abs."

Her eyes go wide. "Really?"

I can admit this to Abigail. Using the notion of teaching a life lesson softens the blow to the gut when I say it out loud. "Yep. See, it's okay to admit we make mistakes sometimes. Even I do."

"Well, did you say sorry?"

She's got me. I fumble a bit over my words before settling on being honest. "You know, I haven't, not really."

Abigail snuggles her bunny and clicks her tongue. "Say sorry Uncle Ro. That's not nice."

I plant a kiss on her forehead and smile. "You're right. It's not nice. Now, to bed, itty, bitty kid."

"I'm nine in four weeks!" The way she says it is a kind of protest she's kept since she turned seven. She is *not* a kid.

I chuckle, and flip out her light from where I stand in the doorway. "Fine, goodnight little kid." She glares and I cant my head to one side. "No? Still? Uh, how about little girl?" Abigail growls. "Fine, okay, okay. Goodnight my awesomely amazing, beautifully smart . . . teenager."

She giggles and smacks her hands onto her mattress. "Nine," she sings. "I'm nine, Uncle Ro."

"Right, right, *almost* nine," I say, "I'll get it straight someday. Love you kid."

"Love you. Oh, Uncle Ro?"

"What?"

"Say sorry to Sloan. I like her. She gave me that smelly stuff that makes me feel better."

I follow her pointed finger to the oil bottle on the dresser. Lavender.

I smile thinking I ought to tease Sloan a little more about being a hippie or something, but the back of my throat is scratchy. I don't know when she took the time to talk to Abigail, let alone teach her how to use the scent to feel calmer, but it matters. More than so many things, simply that she cares matters.

Abigail rolls over, so she faces the wall and just as well. I don't want her to see the dumbstruck expression on my face. She likes Sloan, but so do I. I never stopped.

Downstairs the inn is quiet. Only a standing lamp lights the front lobby, with a wax warmer that smells like pine needles perfuming the space. I keep a fire going until I go to bed, there is something relaxing about the darkness with the flicker of shadows from the flames. Usually, I take a little time to sit alone, and rehash the day. Think about how I can help Abigail, the inn, Jeri, how I can do all this when most days it feels like I have no idea what step to take next.

A soft voice comes from the living room, and I peek around the edge of the open wall. Sloan is sitting in the deep couch in front of the fire. The curls in her hair look a little wild in the ponytail on top of her head, and I can't remember ever loving a hairstyle so much. I dig my fingernails into the meat of my hands.

Don't do that, I think. But I can't help myself. I think a great deal. Things like the way her sweater hugs her narrow shoulders perfectly, the way she wears fuzzy socks rolled way over the top of her leggings like a weirdo. I think of the gentle curve of her neck when she stretches to one side. I think everything until my head hurts.

When Sloan rubs her forehead with her thumb and forefinger, I start to guess who she's talking to. Maybe her dad? Imagining him makes my blood grow too hot. All the while we were running wild, Sloan would go home to be demeaned and berated and she never told me. I knew her parents fought like lions, to the point Sloan would pray they'd get divorced, but I never knew that ire had ever been pointed at her.

"Okay fine, Mom," she mutters.

I free a slow breath. Kristine. I'm good with Kristine.

"I still think this is . . . just, so unfair and really, *really* want you to reconsider. It would mean a lot to me." Sloan pauses while her mom says something. I watch her shoulders slump in disappointment. "No, I get it, and that's nice of you to think of Hallie it's just—" Another pause then, "Okay, love you. Yeah, I will. Bye."

Sloan tosses her phone onto the next cushion and buries her face in her palms. I should go, but I glance at the fire still crackling. I really do need to put it out. With a bit of added noise, I step into the room.

Sloan whips around at the sound of my plodding steps. Her eyes are like pale crystals in the firelight. I noticed as kids, but when I notice now it's like a sucker punch of sudden want.

"Sorry to barge in. I was checking on the fire."

"Oh," she says and snatches her phone. "I can leave."

"It's okay. If you want to stay for a bit." If you want me to stay that would be even better.

She flashes me a preoccupied smile and sits back against the couch. No invitation, so I start to back out of the room.

Sloan peeks over her shoulder. "Where are you going?"

All I can do is shrug.

"Stay awhile," she tells me, facing the flames again. "If you want."

I want. Shoving my hands into the pockets of my jeans I take the awkward, round-about way to the couch and sit on the other end, a good three feet between us. Sloan smiles. I smile. We're so terribly bad at pretending there isn't a ball about to burst with the things we aren't saying.

"How were your calls, the video things?" I ask.

"Oh, good. We're all feeling a little stressed with being blocked from the lodge, but I've got a great team. Everyone is pulling their weight."

"Good," I say as I drag my sweaty palms over my thighs. "That's good."

"Do you like the resort?" she asks, her brow furrowed. "I haven't ever stopped to consider maybe you hate it, and here I am going on about it. I really don't think it'll hurt your business or anything, it's a private resort and—"

"Sloan," I say, stopping her from saying everything in one breath. "I know, I've been to the county meetings about it. I get that it's aimed at like billionaires and their third homes and whatever. Above the caliber the old Holly Berry Inn takes."

She rolls her eyes, but smiles. "Not just billionaires. I mean, millionaires will be there too."

"Oh, right. We can't forget the peasants of the resort. I hope you have plenty of food programs with discounts."

We both laugh for a minute before settling into an easier quiet. Sloan gathers her legs onto the couch, and hugs her knees to her chest, smiling softly as she watches the fire. I can't look anywhere but at her, and she catches me.

"What?" she says with a shy laugh.

I shake my head and recline in the corner of the couch, one arm slung over the back. "Nothing, it's a little weird—you being here, I mean."

"Weird is one word. My mom says it's fate."

I laugh in the back of my throat. "Fate?"

"Yeah." Sloan releases her legs and sits cross-legged on the cushion. "Long, lost friends reuniting is how she put it. But she's into all that stuff, like all roads lead us to our destiny sort of thing."

"And do you believe it?" I don't know why I ask because I don't know if I want to know the answer. What if she's still not pleased to be here. True, I wasn't leaping for joy, but now that I've had a night or two to wade through the fog she brings, if fate brought her here, I'd send fate one of Jeri's gift baskets.

"Do I believe in fate? I don't know. I like having control of my own life."

Right. I tap the back of the couch and force my eyes on the fire. "How is your mom?"

Sloan sighs and picks at the toe of one of her socks. "She's fine. I thought I'd see her next week at the open house, but . . . she's not going to make it now."

"Why? It's sort of your thing, isn't it?" I'm a little ashamed I haven't asked much about what Sloan actually does.

"Yeah. I've worked on the lodge for almost two years."

"Then why isn't she coming?"

Sloan looks at me, her lips set in a bloodless line. "Because my dad and stepmom think it will just cause tension and look bad for our family. They used Hallie as an excuse as if she doesn't have enough of a burden living with my dad. My mom is awesome to Hallie, treats her like another daughter. That says a lot, but now because she cares about her, my mom is going to spend Christmas alone."

"Wait," I say, my eyes narrowed. I adjust so I'm facing her on the couch, one leg tucked underneath me. "Your dad is using your little sister to keep your mom away? That's . . . that's . . ."

"Messed up, I know."

Not the word I wanted to use, but I'm used to keeping my mouth clean around Abigail, I guess. "No offense, but I don't remember your dad being this big of jerk."

"Ah, he just gets better with age," she says sardonically. "Tracy called me this morning too. As a quick reminder that the lodge better be up to snuff, or my father will be embarrassed. He's an investor, you see."

I'm sort of stuck in this weird place, where I want to take her in my arms and make her feel like she's enough, the same as Abigail, and a rougher spot of wanting to punch Shane Hanson in the nose. The way she tangles her fingers together again and again, I opt for something less violent. "That's cool of your mom, since Hallie isn't hers and all."

"Yeah, even cooler since she's her husband's love child, right?"

I tilt my head. "A little crass." True as it is.

Sloan laughs. "Don't worry, I don't tell Hallie the scandalous truth. But the fact that my mom views her for what she is, an innocent kid who got stuck in the center of an ugly divorce and affair, well it makes me love my mom even more. And makes me angry that she's rolling over for him again."

"She shouldn't," I say. "And you should tell her how much it means to you. She'd come for you. Don't hold back, that's what I say."

Sloan smiles, a soft smile. One that builds slowly. "Maybe you're right."

And I'm a hypocrite. My discussion with Abigail rails in my skull. "Leaving things unsaid, well, it causes nothing but problems."

"I guess," she says cautiously.

Be a man. Be an example, for Abigail. This is for her. This is for Sloan. Truth told, this is as much for me as anyone. I shift on my seat and lean over my knees. "Sloan." My voice is stupid. All wrong and rough. I lace my fingers together between my knees. "Can we talk about . . . what happened with us after Jen—"

"It's snowing again." Sloan jumps off the couch as if she's been burned and hurries to the window. She watches the soft snowfall, acting like it's the first she's seen of the stuff. My pulse won't stop thudding. She's avoiding this as much as me. Wrong move, Sloan Hanson. Wrong move.

It's like a primal checkbox dings inside with a pop-up sign that reads: *challenge accepted.*

I stand and cross the room, stopping just behind her. Close enough I can feel the heat of her skin. "Sloan." *Gah.* That rough husky sound again. Blood pulses heat through my palm when I reach out and touch her arm, gently urging her to face me.

"Have you thought about a Christmas tree? You don't have one." Her eyes are pointed at the carpet.

"Uh, yeah. We get one this weekend every year. But Sloan I—"

"I have so many extra decorations at the lodge if you want any. If I ever get up there again, then I'll bring you some."

"Great." I step closer. "Sloan, we need—"

"You know what else might look good—"

I take hold of her shoulders. "Sloan, stop," I say. She bites her bottom lip. "We need to talk."

"We don't need to do this," she whispers. She hugs herself, barring me away. Each breath she takes is fast and harsh. Like she's terrified.

"What are you afraid of?" What have I been afraid of? Sloan standing so near, all I can think is how I'm an idiot who should've tried to get this woman back in my life years ago. "The Sloan I knew would've given me an earful by now about how stupid I've been."

"That girl doesn't exist anymore."

She says it with such finality, I feel a tight cramp in my chest. She starts to walk away. This is all wrong, it was supposed to be simple. Like riding a bike, we'd pick up the easy, talk about anything relationship we had as kids. I'm grappling for anything to keep her in the room.

"I'm sorry." I say it so fast, I'm not sure I even separated the words.

She pauses in front of the mantle. "Sorry for what?"

I close my eyes and drift next to her. "For that day, for what I said."

"We were both hurting, Rowan. I know I can't compare to what it felt like to lose a sister, but I was scared to leave you and that is exactly what was happening. Moving away to live with my dad, I didn't want to leave you. So, I blurted all that out. We don't need to go over it again. It's done. We have different lives."

She starts to retreat again, and I watch. What can I say? She's right. We do have different lives, we learned to live without each other. Maybe that's where this ought to stay.

But watching her leave my side now, all I can do is remember that day. I'll never forget the moment when my heart shot to my throat, when I stammered for the words, when fear took hold and I said all the wrong things.

Christmas Past

Chapter 8

Sloan

December 23, 2012

I leave the bathroom, my stomach an empty, gaping hole still filled with acid and sick. My throat is raw, my eyes are puffy, and they sting.

This isn't happening.

Wiping my eyes, I stomp down the stairs and return to the living room. The voices are harsh, sharp, and unwelcoming. I want to disappear, want the old hardwood floor to swallow me whole. Outside the world is bleak. Gray skies threaten to dump another heap of snow over the town, and I don't care. A week ago I watched my best friend put his sister in the ground, and now . . . my lip quivers. How will I face Rowan with this?

I hardly lift my feet as I trudge back into the living room.

Mom is standing at the bay window, hugging her middle with one arm, while chewing on her opposite thumb. She glances her sympathy, her broken heart, my way.

Dad, on the other hand, is more interested in his fancy wristwatch and huffs his annoyance. "Are we finished with the temper tantrums, Sloan

Marie?"

"I'm not going," I say, voice raw.

My dad narrows his sharp, blue eyes. "You don't have a choice."

"Mom," I beg. Everything is breaking all over again. "Please. I-I-I've lived with you for three years now, please don't make me leave everything right before my senior year."

"Oh, honey," she says.

"Kristine, don't baby her."

For once, my mother shoots my father with a glare and takes me in her arms. "This time I agree with your dad, as hard as it is. Sweetie, I'm going to be on the road so much these next few months—you deserve more than that, and this school, it's amazing. It's one year. One measly year, then you can see the world, reach for those stars and all that jazz."

I bury my face in my mother's neck. It's more than a year. It's eighteen months of not seeing her. I know my dad, and I know his wife. They'll keep me wrapped up in their fancy parties and events, so I'll be lucky if I see Mom for a second on President's Day or some holiday no one remembers.

"My friends are here, you're here."

She squeezes me tighter. "Sweetie, I'm not *going* to be here, that's the point. And . . . and I know this is terrible timing, but Ro . . . you guys will always be Sloan and Rowan. It's maybe eight hours in the car, hon. Eight, nothing hours."

She's trying to paint the pretty picture, but the idea of living out our senior year, one where we'd already devised the cleverest of senior pranks involving vegetable oil and misnumbered chickens, one where we'd agreed to go to senior prom together is so wrong it's disgusting. Senior year, when I promised I'd let Rowan drive my new jeep every day if he took Adult Life class with me, and wore the pregnant belly, and took care of the dolls that cry. He agreed. Doesn't my dad know how much coercing that took? Senior year is the year Rowan told me we'd do the famous Silver Creek True Senior dare, where couples line up on the fifty-yard line and lock lips. Whoever lasts the longest becomes legend, and gets their name painted on the Senior wall on the side of the bleachers. Over a decade of being joined at the hip, why not be joined at the lips for a night. My stomach cramps, like I might throw up again, at the thought of Rowan taking Eva to the football field instead of me.

"I'm not going."

"You are going," Dad snaps. "You are moving to Cottonwood with me, with Tracy, and you'll not throw a fit. Hallie doesn't need to see her older sister acting younger than her."

Mom winces. She's amazing with Hallie, but I know the sweet little four-year-old is still a reminder of my dad's betrayal, and now because she reacted, my angel mother will probably feel guilty for it.

"Why are you doing this!" I shout it to them both. I don't care who answers.

"Sloan," Mom says with more firmness. "I need you to be brave and do this. I need this job, babe, and I need you to be safe, with your family." She cups my face in her hands. "Think of it as a year before college that you get to really be with your sister before you go out into the world."

I love Hallie. I do, but I love my mother too. I love Rowan. My heart is nothing more than a crushed mess of sharp, jagged pieces.

I love Rowan Graham.

And I'm leaving.

He deserves—no—he *needs* to know.

Chapter 9

Rowan

December 24, 2012

The house is too quiet.

Mom hasn't even left her room yet, and Dad, well, he's been out in the shed since I woke up.

We don't know how to be a family right now. Not with Jenny gone. I dig my fingers into my eyes when the sting comes again. I'm so sick of crying. So sick of hurting. So sick of . . . everything. I can't wait to get out of here, to travel with the Army, soldier my way through business school and make something of myself away from memories of my sister. Even when I went with Dad to pay utilities yesterday Jenny was there. Why did Mom sign her up for the Miss Silver Creek pageant four years ago? Now her picture is going to hang in the city building forever.

The only good thing, the single bright spot, is Sloan said she'd go to school wherever I get stationed. She even promised if I went somewhere nuts like Germany or Japan she'd work at some pub or teach English until I was finished.

Sounds extreme, but knowing Sloan, she's already working on her visa and passport. Just in case.

Outside the rest of the town has moved on with Christmas Eve and I hate them. I hate them so much. Don't they know life is supposed to stop. Don't they *remember* that Jenny . . . that she's dead? How can they celebrate something fleeting like Christmas at a time like this?

Upstairs I hear my mom moving around, waking from her comatose grief. I rub my forehead; I shouldn't think things like that. My mom has been the rock for all of us through this. She's allowed time to crumble especially since Scott said he'll be staying with his parents this year for the holidays. We won't even see Abigail on her first Christmas.

"Hi sweetie," Mom's hoarse voice says at my back.

I look over my shoulder. She's in her bathrobe, eyes swollen, her graying hair is in a messy ponytail, but I smile. She's holding baking supplies. Traditional candy cane pancakes. Every Christmas Eve.

"Mom," I whisper. "You don't need to. Not this year."

She hiccups and braces over the counter, nodding frantically. "Yes . . . yes I do. I need to feel like she's . . . like she's coming. Like it's . . . normal."

I forget myself for half a second and go to my mom. Alarmed in that I've never seen her sobbing like this. Before she can curl to the ground, I hold her tightly, squeezing her. I'm taller now, so it's not hard to do. Crying together is how Dad finds us. He bear hugs us both, and I don't know how we stay standing all of us sniffing, crying, and snotting on each other.

But that's how Sloan finds us too.

"Oh."

I snap my head out of our family circle and see her in the frame of the sliding glass door at the back of the house. Her eyes are swollen too. Great. We're all crying.

She takes a step back into the snow. "Sorry," she whispers.

My mom catches her eye. "Oh, Sloanie, come in. You're bound to catch us melting in a few puddles for the rest of time. Come in."

I see tears in her eyes when she hesitantly crosses into our kitchen and squeezes my mom, whispering things I can't hear, but it's enough that my mom cracks a watery smile and strokes Sloan's short curly hair.

I hurry and wipe my eyes with the back of my hand and clear my throat. I'm not embarrassed she caught me crying, Sloan's seen that enough lately. I don't think I'd make it through any of this without Sloan Hanson.

She slides her arm through mine, as she often does, squeezes, then leans her head against my shoulder. I rest my cheek on top of hers. And we stay there for a quiet moment watching my mom smile and tell us how glad she is to have another reason to make our traditional Christmas Eve breakfast. She insists making the pancakes helps, even if she's crying, it helps.

Sloan stays. We eat pancakes filled with crumbles of peppermint and topped with maple syrup. Dad laughs as he drizzles heaping globs of whipped cream over the top, then adds sprinkles in the shape of snowflakes. At the end, we're smiling and laughing about memories with

Jenny and my heart doesn't break as much. Sloan insists she be the one to clean up. I mean, I stay and help, I'm not totally oblivious, and I think my mom and dad are grateful to have a moment alone.

I don't need to say anything to Sloan, she knows what I'm feeling and the little squeezes she gives my arm when she walks by are enough for a little while.

"Don't you need to be with your mom?" I ask when it starts getting dark outside. Sloan is reading a *Popular Mechanics* magazine, twisting in my computer chair while I am sprawled out on my bed, doing nothing but staring at the ceiling. Her breath catches and I see the flinch in her jaw. "Whoa, what's up?"

She scoffs as I sit up and crosses the room. Sloan starts smoothing out my hair standing on end, but I see the glisten of tears in her eyes.

Maybe it's Jenny. I get that. Sometimes I start crying for no reason too. I pinch her arm. "What's wrong?"

Sloan's chin quivers and she looks to the ground. "I need to tell you something."

"Okay," I say slowly.

"Can we go for a walk?"

"It's freezing."

"I know. Wear a coat."

I roll my eyes, but obey. Sloan drags out a snow hat with a puff ball on top from her pocket and slides it over her head. I shove my hands in my pockets and zip my coat up under my chin. If her skinny butt can handle the cold, so can I.

We walk down the street, stopping at the end of the road when it opens into the park. Sloan leans against the waist-high fence and stares at the slides covered in three feet of snow.

"What's up?" I say, bouncing on my toes to keep warm.

Sloan drags in a shuddering breath. Holy cow, she's crying a lot. "Um . . ."

"Hey," I say, nudging her ribs with my elbow when she doesn't go on. "I know this is hard, trust me I get it."

She shakes her head. "I miss Jenny, and I . . . I think losing her makes this, it makes it so much worse, Ro."

Now my fingers are numb, but I don't think it's because of the cold. Something is up. "What's going on? You're freaking me out."

Sloan doesn't cry easily. When she dated that idiot Ian Hicks, and when he broke up with her in front of half the cafeteria, Sloan didn't run out in embarrassment. No, she smashed his face with her greasy pizza as she walked by and said, "Don't be too embarrassed you couldn't handle me."

I'm pretty sure she earned a standing ovation. But right here, she's almost hyperventilating.

I take her arm and wheel her around. "Sloan, what's wrong?"

Her head has always fit under mine, but in this moment, I take note of how perfectly it does. Her arms are around my waist, and she's holding on like I'm the only solid thing left.

"My dad," she starts in a breathy gasp. "My mom and dad are making me . . . they're making me move in with . . . him and Tracy."

It takes at least five seconds for what she's saying to sink in. When it does, my stomach turns sour and angry. Out of instinct, I draw her in closer, as if I can keep her dad from stealing her from me. "No." A lame response, that comes out in a rough croak. But I shake my head. I refuse to believe this and the spinning in my head draws it out again. "No."

Sloan loses it against my coat. I'm like stone, hard and unmoving. I'm furious at her dad, at her mom, at Jenny for leaving, at Sloan for not fighting. I'm angry enough at everything that I can't even cry.

When she pulls back, her face is red and wet.

I glare at her and ask, "When?"

"After the new year."

I swear under my breath. I don't cuss often, but this moment certainly calls for it. Sloan doesn't flinch. I lean over the fence on my elbows, covering my face with my palms to keep from screaming my frustration with life. Then I jolt up. "No, stay with me. You could live with us. You know you could. Stay with us, please."

I sound like a wimp, but I can beg with Sloan. She won't tease me about it.

She drags in another shuddering breath again and her face contorts like she's eaten something sour, and I understand. "You've already asked, haven't you?"

"It was my first compromise. My dad . . . he just wants to win and force me into some stupid private school, so it looks like he has some princess for a kid. And my mom, she's agreeing!"

Sloan goes into how her mom will be gone for six months out of the year, but honestly, I'm not listening. More than ever I want to disappear from this place. I want to leave and never look back. How do I go through a day without knowing Crazy Sloan Hanson, my best friend, will be there with me? We have other friends, she has her tennis girls, I have my basketball teammates. But everyone knows, where Sloan goes, I go.

I feel myself starting to wall up, and even take a step away from her. Things will hurt less if I put some distance between us, right? Feeling nothing will make waking up without my sister and without Sloan at least doable until I can kiss the memories of this town goodbye for good.

"Rowan," she says.

"Yeah," I say flatly.

She hiccups. "I need to tell you something before I go."

"Then tell me." I can't do this, can't pretend like this doesn't kill like burying my sister did. My mom tells me I'm the king at closing off, and she's right. I don't even feel the cold of the night anymore.

Sloan takes my hand, our skin warm where it touches. She meets my eyes. "You are my best friend," she says softly.

Another wall goes up. I can't do this. Not now. Do this maybe, *maybe*, six months from now and I might be less stuck in this constant grief, but not now. I'd rather flip the switch into blank stares and hardened nothingness. And I do. That is exactly what I do.

Sloan steps closer. "But I—" She hesitates. "I think I love you . . . more than that."

What is she saying? My brow furrows. Did she—wait. Did Sloan just tell me she had feelings for me? Feelings I've had since we turned fourteen? And tonight, the night I am a cold block of hatred and anger and resentment, tonight she decides to tell me? Tell me this last summer, or heck, even two months ago and I'd say something, *do* something. Now, I just stand still and furious. I turned off and tuned out of any warmth. I'm just . . . angry.

"Ro," she whimpers and takes my arm. I meet her wanting eyes with a steely glare. "Do you have anything to say to that? I-I just told you I love you."

Looking back, I understand where the words came from. A place of a grieving, bitter, terrified teenager. I meet Sloan's eyes and say, "And what do you expect me to do with that?"

She backs away as if I slapped her in the face. "Nothing," she says. "We just tell each other things, and you deserved . . . deserved to know."

"Yeah, we told each other things when you lived here. But in a week, you won't."

She sniffs. "So that's all it takes for you not to be my friend anymore? I move away? Last I checked we both have driver's licenses, and my mom will still be here sometimes. I'm not moving to a new country."

"I don't want to do this," I admit and start stomping back toward my house.

"That's it? That's all you have to say to me, I mean turn me down if you want, but I thought you'd have something to say when your best friend tells you she is in love with you."

"I don't want to be in love!" I shout. Sloan skids to a stop, eyes wide. "Not with you, not with anyone!"

"Fine! What do you want?"

To not feel. I want Jenny back. I want you to stay here. I love you back and I'm scared I'll lose you too. All the thoughts I can't say tumble like a knot of barbed wire in my head. Fury and hurt and fear take hold and I find more comfort pushing everything away than wallowing in this agony I can't shake. "I want to be done with all of this," I tell her. "I want to leave, join the army and . . . forget *everything* about his place! Alone."

"Wait," she says. "You don't . . . are you saying you don't want me around at all? What about after graduation? We had plans together."

"No, they're my plans," I say. "And you should have your own."

"Rowan—"

"I think," I say slowly. Am I really saying this? The rational side of my brain is begging me to stop, but the hurt, wretched side punches that side into submission. “I think . . . I don’t think we should talk anymore. It’ll be easier. Kind of like a band aid goodbye.”

I might as well have slugged her in the gut the way she looks at me. “You don’t mean that.”

“I do,” I say. “I’m going inside now. This is better, it’ll be easier this way.”

“For you? Because this isn’t easier for me. You’re not thinking straight.”

I keep walking.

“Fine!” she screams at my back. “I’ll leave you alone, but I’m still here, Rowan. I’ll always be there for you. I’ll wait for you to get your stupid head right.”

I hear her cry at my back, but I don’t stop.

I can’t stop or I’ll just . . . I’ll break.

Christmas Present

Chapter 10

Rowan

Sloan is nearly out of the living room. Everything about that night flashes through my head, like a waking nightmare.

I can still hear her crying, the tremble in her voice when she told me she loved me. The way I went numb and hid the secret way I'd always noticed Sloan flicked her pencil when she was concentrating, or how she shrugged at her reflection whenever she fixed her hair, as if saying 'well, this is what we have to work with'. I remember the hot, jagged knife it was to my heart to shut her out because if I loved her back, if I let her go admitting I loved her, then there was the risk I'd lose her like I lost Jenny. That night, that entire year I couldn't stomach another heartbreak.

But it's not that night now.

It's not that year. Eight years later, and I still fumble around Sloan. My pulse still races. Fear is not going to separate us again.

I cross the distance between us and take her arm. She spins around, eyes wide. We're chest to chest.

"Stop," I whisper. I feel her heartbeat beat against my body. Her eyes bounce between mine, searching. Slowly, I drag my hand up her arm until my calloused palm rests against the softness of her neck. "What I said, it was more than hurting over my sister, Sloan. Maybe that's what I hid behind, but what it came down to was fear of opening a new piece of you and me, then losing it someday. Which is stupid because I shoved you away anyway."

She breathes hard. I shudder when her hand covers mine on her neck. "Why did you cut me out? I would've had you any way I could get." Her voice is soft, timid, and I deserve it.

I close my eyes and take the risk that comes with unhindered, honesty. "I first noticed you as more than my friend at your fourteenth birthday party. When you hugged me for getting you that—"

"Yearly movie pass," she says, her thumb running over the back of my hand. "I think that was for you too since we always went together."

"Maybe." I weave my arm around her waist, expecting her to pull away, but reveling when she arches against me. "When you went to homecoming with stupid Tyson Riggs, I faked sick because I didn't want to see him all over you."

"You did not."

"I did."

"I faked sick too," she admits. "We left at eight because it was so boring without you there."

I crack a smile. "That's mean, Sloan."

I'm hyper aware of her second hand on my chest, the way her fingers trace the button line of my shirt. "You're apologizing, Rowan. You don't get to judge me. Keep going."

I take a deep breath. "That night, when I said those things, I wanted to just *not feel.* Jenny was gone and it felt like it would be you next."

"I get that now—"

I trap her face between both my hands, enjoying the way she gasps softly. "I'm not finished. You still interrupt all the time." Her cheeks shift under my palms when she smiles. "I'm sorry for hurting you that night, Sloan. I regretted it, but I never had the nerve to tell you. I spiraled after you left, and didn't live . . . as I should've."

She presses against me, her touch gentle.

"By the time I got my head on straight and cleaned up my act, so much time had passed."

"I should've called—"

"Woman," I say with a smile, our faces closer. "Would you let me get this out?"

Sloan's fingertips are on my jawline when she grins. "You keep pausing."

Little sparks of heat follow everywhere she touches. Feelings I've hidden for years break free, thoughts and wants I've kept since she barreled back into my life heat my blood. All I need is to be as close to this woman as I can get, and even then, it won't be enough.

"When Abigail came to me," I say softly. "I was terrified, and the only person I thought of was you. I tried to reach you, even dug deep enough and called your office."

Sloan's eyes widen. "I never got any messages, Rowan. I would've called you."

My thumb brushes over her cheek. "I know. I'm trying to tell you I've regretted pushing you away this long."

My fingers thread through her ponytail, I study the curls for a moment, the shape of her brows, her eyes. Sloan holds her breath. Her fingers run around my back, brushing each divot of my spine.

My voice is hardly more than a whisper. "I've wanted a do-over for eight years, a chance to tell you that I did want you then." I nudge her chin with my index finger knuckle, so her face tilts toward mine. Her body feels good —so good—against mine. "And I've been given the chance to tell you, Sloan, that I *still* want you."

A pause is all I can afford. One simple moment to memorize everything about her eyes, her pink lips, the firelight on her cheeks before my mouth crushes hers.

Sloan frees a soft noise, but gives into my kiss in another heartbeat. Her long fingers drag through my hair, holding the back of my head, keeping my mouth firmly on hers. Her lips are soft, amazingly soft, and she tastes sweet. One kiss slides to the next as I walk her back against the wall. I brace with one palm open near her head, my arm keeping her body against mine as I reacquaint myself with Sloan Hanson in the most stunning ways.

We've never kissed. Once at a party we came close, but both chickened out at the last minute. What a shame, and clearly, I'm an idiot. *This* is what I've been missing all this time?

My hand travels the curve of her waist. Her fingers dance along the back of my neck, teasing the skin under the collar of my shirt. I could kiss her all night, hold her against my heart until the earth stopped spinning, so when we break apart it's too soon.

Sloan's eyes are closed, her lips swollen and perfect. I bring my forehead to hers, breathing heavily, my hand still possessively holding her waist.

"Have I told you," she gasps as she curls her arm around the back of my neck, "how much I've missed you?"

I smile and drag my thumb across her bottom lip until I feel her shiver against me. With a flick of my brow, I dip my head again, and say, "Not nearly enough."

Chapter 11

Sloan

Sunlight stirs me from sleep. I crack my eyes and stare at the gilded ribbons weaving across the bed and carpet. Slumped across the mattress on my stomach, I hug my pillow tightly against my body as my mouth curls up into a shy smile. My fingertips touch my lips as though the tingle of Rowan's kiss is still there hours later.

Rowan Graham kissed me. I kissed him. Many times, thank you very much.

I can hardly keep up with the whirlwind that happened last night, and truth told, I'm not sure I want to keep up. My stomach twists as I think of the way his hands brushed my face, held my waist, played with my hair. I sink deeper into the blankets, content to remain there all morning replaying each delicious moment. Part of me always knew Rowan was a good kisser. I'd seen him with his girlfriends in high school, and frankly, girls talk. Putting makeup on in the locker room after gym class, or drifting the hallways between classes I heard things. My stomach knotted then, more in jealousy I was too afraid to face, but now those knots are mine. I am *finally* that girl who'd be gossiping with her friends at the perfection of that mouth.

My blood jolts to my head. I'll see him this morning. Obviously, being that I'm staying at his inn, but how am I supposed to act? It's not just about Rowan and me anymore, now is it. There is Abigail to think of. A little girl who's been through enough heartache and doesn't need an ounce more.

I need to look at Rowan as her father, right? Does that mean he'll want to keep this slow? Probably wise. Then again, does it mean there is anything to even keep slow? His interests will rightly be about Abigail's feelings, and maybe he isn't ready to have a third party in their dynamic duo. Last night might've been us being caught up in a romantic moment.

I grunt some frustration at myself and kick off the bedspread.

It was a kiss, an addicting kiss, but still a kiss. It's not like he asked me to be his girlfriend. We're adults, and sometimes adults kiss with no strings attached. I don't need him to define anything, and it ought to be enough to say Rowan is back in my life. Missing the chunk of my heart he took with him is over, and that's enough.

I bite my bottom lip halfway through applying my eyeliner. Enough. Okay, having him back is enough, but I'm not sure one kiss will be enough.

Even dating Luke for three years, I don't ever remember being so embroiled in a moment; I couldn't breathe or think straight. The way Rowan's mouth claimed mine, aggressively, then slowly, gently. I shake thoughts of him away, if I don't, then I'll never finish getting ready and I'll be stewing in front of this mirror all day.

Sliding my sweater over my head I hear the faint buzz of my phone. The muffled noise comes from somewhere in the tangle of quilts and sheets in my unmade bed. When I find the bright screen it goes black the same moment my fingers curl around the phone. I don't need to wait long before Luke's name flashes brightly with a second call.

My jaw is tight when I answer. "Luke, good morning." We're so formal now, well, I am formal with him. He would like to keep me eating from the palm of his hand, but the problem with that is I wouldn't be the only one.

"Sloan," he says sharply. "Where in the h—" He pauses, and I hear voices near him that likely cause him to keep from cursing. He softens his voice and corrects. "Where have you been? I've emailed you and now called several times. I was starting to think you'd frozen to death up there."

"I'm at the Holly Berry Inn," I say as I tug on my ankle boots. "The road to the upper canyon has been closed. I've held staff meetings over video calls, Luke. We're fine."

He chuffs his annoyance. "Fine? Sloan the open house is just over a week away, and I've been here, thinking my property manager is missing. It is not fine."

I roll my eyes. "Luke, what do you expect? I doubt the plumbers were even able to get up there."

"True," he admits. "But that's why I've been searching for you like crazy this morning. They called with an update. From the lodge. The roads must be open if they're there, right?"

The roads are open. I slide off the bed and peek outside. It didn't snow last night based on the packed parking lot, and the sun is glaring viciously off the snow. My shoulders slump. I'll need to be on my way then. A brutal reminder this was never meant to be permanent.

"Yeah, it's nice up here today," I admit softly.

"Okay," Luke says with a touch of relief. "So, you'll get to the lodge and make sure everything is in place for the party?"

"No, I think I'll take my time."

"*Sloan*," he warns.

"You walked right into that. Calm down. This is my part of the job, Luke."

I can practically hear him rolling his eyes. "This is what we've been working toward, forgive me for being a little uptight about it all."

"Sorry," I tell him because he's right. This isn't Luke being annoyingly possessive, this is his job. My job. My chance to leave and take my permanent position.

Like I always wanted.

I want it. Right?

"I'll check in as soon as I get an update on the progress," I tell him.

"Okay," he says. "I'll make sure you have a room set up at the lodge. I'm sure you've been going crazy trapped in that place." He chuckles, but I can't even fake a laugh to appease him. Luke doesn't notice and in the background it sounds as though he's typing.

"I'll be in touch," I finally say.

"Thanks. I'm glad you're alive. Oh, by the way Tracy called to tell me they're excited to stay in the Gold suite. You didn't hold back with their reservation, did you?"

"Well, as you and my dad always remind me, he is a top investor."

Luke laughs. "True. Tracy said Shane apparently wants to go out with us one night, talk plans and catch up. Should we take them to *Paysha Grill* or *Fanelli's*?"

"Wait, what?"

Luke's voice has an edge to it, like my question annoys him. "Dinner. Where do you want to eat dinner when your family comes?"

"Why do they want to eat with us together?" I don't mean to sound as growly as I do, but I can't get over how much my family keeps Luke in our lives. Like they are on his side even after what he did.

"Because they love me," he says with a laugh. "Come on, we can still eat together, right?"

"That's not a good idea."

"Because I might win you over again? Would that be the worst thing?"

Yes. My voice cracks. "I'm not into sharing, Luke."

He sighs loudly. "Here we go," he says under his breath. "Okay, Sloan. Someday you'll believe me when I say I made a mistake, and let it go. Until then, I'll look for your call. And I say we go to Paysha's. Good steak."

I end the call without a goodbye. My stomach turns sour. They are all so . . . pretentious and assuming. So typical. Luke is the VP, Dad the investor. Business comes first.

I imagine the horror of my dad's face if I showed up to a fancy dinner with Rowan. Hopefully he'd wear his jeans and leather boots, maybe I'd tell him not to shave his beard, let it grow wild for a few days.

I laugh at the thought and keep my smile all the way down to the dining room.

A group of five men in burly coats and snow boots crowd around a table. Jeri is laughing with them as she pours coffee into their mugs. She waves me in and gestures to the corner. My insides warm the moment I catch sight of Rowan. He sits at the table, leaning over a paper with Abigail. I lick my lips and hold my breath as I cross the space. Rowan catches my eye, and a shy grin tugs at the corner of his mouth. I feel as though every inch of me is on fire. Doubtless, my face is nothing but a wash of pink.

"What's all this?" I ask Abigail as my grand icebreaker.

"Spelling words," she tells me a little like a lament. "I'm not good at spelling."

"No?" I say as I take a seat. "You want to know a secret about being a good speller?"

Abigail lifts her brows and nods vigorously.

"Reading," I tell her.

"I like when we read at night."

"Does your uncle read to you? Or do you read to him?'

She flushes. "I start, but then I make him read to me."

"And I'm sure he caves whenever you flash that cute smile." I tickle her cheek until she giggles. Rowan smiles, but doesn't disagree.

"I'll bring you my favorite book when I was nine, and you start reading to him. I bet you a bucket of gummy bears spelling will get a whole lot easier."

Abigail beams at Rowan and whispers, "She knows I like gummy bears."

He leans closer to his niece. "Sloan used to be made of gummy bears."

"Well, they are the best kind of candy," I say with a knowing glance at Abigail. The way she smiles I safely assume she agrees.

Jeri joins us at the table, handing me a plate of pumpkin pancakes and tea bags while she digs into her own breakfast. "Another group will be here tonight," she tells Rowan. "That'll fill the rooms."

"Oh, uh," I say. I didn't think it would feel so wrong to say the simple words I'm leaving, but it does. "The roads to the lodge are open."

Jeri pauses midbite, and Rowan glances at me for half a heartbeat as he helps Abigail with her backpack.

"Wait, you're leaving?" Abigail is the one to ask.

I avoid Rowan's gaze and face her. "I'll still bring the book to you, but my company is going to set me up at the lodge."

My pulses thuds in the back of my throat. Palms are sweaty. I can sense Rowan's eyes boring into me, but can't find the guts to face him.

Abigail pouts. "I wanted to read to you. Uncle Ro always falls asleep."

Praise to this little girl. We all laugh and I dare look across the table. Rowan is facing Abigail, but his eyes flick to me as he says, "Abs, Sloan probably wants to stay up at the lodge. She designed it."

"Oh, kiddo," Jeri says as gleam of yellow passes by the window, "bus is here."

Abigail gulps another drink of chocolate milk before tapping Rowan's arm. "You should still tell her to stay here." She waves at both me and Jeri before darting out of the inn. Rowan watches through the window to make sure she's loaded on the bus before relaxing in his chair.

"I can keep the room open," Jeri suggests.

I smile, not knowing what to say. It's great that Abigail and Jeri want me to stay, but Rowan hasn't said anything. And I do have a job. I'm not on vacation. "Thanks for breakfast," I say tilting the conversation a different direction. "Now that the roads are open, I better get up there."

"I'll take you."

My heart skips a beat when Rowan stands. Jeri lifts a brow, her lips in a tight line, but her eyes are laughing.

"Rowan," I say with a chuckle. "I have a perfectly good rental car right outside."

Jeri gathers our plates, glides next to me, and whispers, "Let the man take you, and I think I've figured out what sort of battle this is."

Rowan glares at the cook as she winks at him, but he grabs his coat from the back of his chair, readying to make the walk out in the cold.

"Don't you have things to do here?" I ask when we're alone.

"Not much. With the storm, I got a lot done when no one was coming. I've got a few hours and I'd like to see what you've done up there. Scope out the competition."

I laugh because the lodge is not his competition. A completely different target market will stay at the lodge, but with any luck Holly Berry will gain more clientele since the private resort does plan to host several public events each year.

But the notion that he wants to see the lodge strikes me. Fiercely. I like that he has an interest in what I do. Enough that a sticky bulge of emotion takes root in the back of my throat. No one outside of my mom has given my work much thought. Luke's only interest in my success is because it'll reflect on his leadership, the same can be said for my dad.

My smile comes on its own. "Okay," I agree softly. "But what about my car?"

Rowan's hand is on the small of my back and I swallow a moan before I embarrass myself. He dips his head next to mine. "Don't worry about the car."

I won't. I plan not to worry about anything today except ways to keep Rowan's hands on me.

Chapter 12

Rowan

Roads opening did little to distress my morning until sitting at the table, hearing Sloan talk about leaving, an unfamiliar need to keep her took hold. An offer to drive up the canyon sort of slipped out as a side effect, but standing outside the massive cabin-style lodge now, I'm glad I came.

"Coming?"

Sloan stands at the wide, thick, hand-carved doors on the front porch. She peeks at me over her shoulder, and the way the sun strikes her face, her eyes look like sapphires. All I can think about is the way those eyes looked at me in the dim living room, our mouths close, our bodies even closer.

I nod and hurry up the stairs to her side. She smiles at me shyly, strange for her. Sloan was never shy around me, in fact, she was too open. I knew things about my female friend most guys preferred to pretend didn't exist. She even had a code word. When I got the text: *hot packs and cookies* that was my cue to come over to watch TV on the couch and not complain about whatever show she picked.

But we aren't the same as back then. Not even close. Maybe I'm a little nervous around her too.

When the doors open, I'm glad for the distraction.

Inside is rustic and enormous. Everything smells like coffee and cinnamon, spice and pine. There are chandeliers made from rough-cut iron that hang in a neat row across the rib of the ceiling. Thick beams crisscross overhead, and at least three spaces the size of the Holly Berry's living room make up one great room. Sectional sofas, reclining chairs and varnished log benches block out each separate space where groups can gather. There are coffee and tea carts scattered throughout, a hospitality desk three times the size as ours. The staircases are wide and filled with housekeepers running towels up and down.

"Wow," I say and I mean it.

"What do you think?"

"You did all this?" I keep my hands in my pockets and drift, spinning to see everything, until I'm standing near the twelve-foot Christmas tree in the center of the room. Three employees are decorating the lower boughs, and another is dragging a ladder over to hit the top branches.

"Well," Sloan says, swinging her arms. "I have a great team, there is no way I did this on my own."

"Don't listen to her," a decorator tells me. "This is Sloan's vision, we're just the extra hands to make it reality."

I grin. Sloan hurries and rolls her eyes, but I think she's trying to hide the way she's blushing.

"Thanks, Sarah, but I don't handle the raises, so you can stop kissing my butt."

The woman hanging red striped ornaments chuckles. "No, I'm just saying the truth. If you want to see butt-kissing, wait until Luke shows up and I'll be like a leech he can't shake."

Sloan flinches. I'm curious, but she buries any disquiet when she takes my arm.

"Come on," she says. "I want to show you the kitchens so you can see what you need to get for Jeri. The woman is a goddess in the kitchen and deserves some pampering by her boss."

"Yeah, I don't think my budget is the same as this place."

"That's why I'm here. I'm going to blow your mind by my classy-chic bargain shopping."

Jeri would ditch me in a heartbeat if she saw the kitchen of the lodge. Stainless steel, granite countertops, smooth wood carving blocks. Sloan demonstrates a few of the appliances that she says Jeri deserves and tells me she has a contact in an overstock appliance center where they get scratch and dents. She's good at selling because I feel like I'm ready to set up a remodel by the time we're heading upstairs to check out the rooms. Sloan is showing me around, but checking things off her own list. At least that's how she puts it.

Inspections of the beds, all at least queen sized with log headboards; all rooms have deep bathtubs and fancy showers. She checks the vents, and drapes. Checks the plumbing in some rooms, then shoots a text to the a few workers and delegates the rest. Sloan drags me along as she speaks with the manager of hospitality. The woman reminds me of my mom, natural gray in her hair, and a warm smile.

"Rowan," Sloan says, shaking me from my admiration of a canvas painting of the Silver Creek scenery.

"Yeah?"

"Maybe you can help. Moreen is already dealing with a frustrated customer who wants to cancel, and she did, but now they are demanding the deposit back too."

"Is the refund policy clearly stated?" I ask.

Moreen nods and pushes up her glasses. "Right on the purchase page, and we have a tab on our website that is specifically for refunds, and it is on the frequently asked questions page."

Sloan smiles and takes a step back. My chest goes tight, taking over like this, but she offers an encouraging nod.

"Well," I start slowly. "We always try to keep people appeased, but with an excuse to take their money still."

Sloan chuckles, but Moreen tilts her head. "I don't understand."

"We give a voucher for the same amount as a reservation deposit, plus a gift card to a local restaurant or something. That way it encourages them to come and stay again. People want cash, but they also like to feel like they're getting a bargain. Even millionaires like a deal," I say with a smirk at Sloan.

She mouths *billionaires* in return and offers me a smug glance. I want to kiss her. Simple as that.

"I like it," Moreen whispers. "Do you give them a time frame?"

I shake my head. "No, we leave it open-ended. Sometimes people need to cancel because an emergency happened, not because they didn't want to come. They can save it and come back whenever they're able."

"And you've had success with it?"

"Yeah, I'm no statistician, but I've figured I get about an eighty-five to ninety percent return rate from those vouchers."

"Wow," Moreen says, beaming at Sloan. "I'd say that's a good thing to try."

Sloan closes the space between us when Moreen scurries away. The tops of our knuckles brush and my head grows foggy when Sloan props her chin on the edge of my shoulder.

"I want to poach you from your own inn and have you handle all this."

I don't give much thought before lacing our fingers together, sparing another glance at the grandness of the space before pulling her closer, so our noses touch. "I'd say you've done amazing all on your own."

She smiles and stands on her toes until our lips brush, but never finishes the job. A whisper of a touch. A rumble sounds in the back of my throat. Teasing me is not going to go over well, not when she's standing this near to me, not when she looks at me like that. She seems rather pleased taunting me with all that she is. So when I smash our lips together, I take a bit of pride in the way she gasps in my mouth.

Her lips part, inviting me to kiss her deeper, and I do. Not long enough, of course, but I have a bit of brain power to remember we're in public, and she's technically at work. Still, she's flushed when I pull away. Mission accomplished.

"I am so mad at you," she whispers against my skin.

"For what?"

She narrows her eyes, voice like honey. "For being stupid and not kissing me eight years ago. Now, I'm all flustered at what I've been missing."

I laugh and take her hand again as she pulls me back to the stairs. "Trust me, I've been kicking myself all night.

Later, Sloan feeds us, giving me an exclusive glimpse at the Christmas Eve buffet specials. The pot roast and stuffed potatoes earn my thumbs up. I even try the vegan asparagus casserole and want seconds.

But I keep peeking at my watch, wishing the afternoon wasn't fleeting. Abigail will be home in thirty minutes and she doesn't like coming home to an empty inn, even if Jeri is usually around.

"I bet Abby will be home soon, huh?"

Sloan surprises me. She's watching the massive clock in the great room. Something burns inside my chest. She thought of Abigail on her own, and that means more than I expected.

"Yeah," I say. "She'll be home soon."

Sloan bites her bottom lip. "Well, do you mind taking me back so I can get my stuff and my car?"

"Stay," I whisper, voice raw. "Stay with us. I'll drive you up here every day if you want, or you can drive, but just stay."

It's not fair of me to ask. The lodge is a massive project, and she's amazing for all she's done. Tension breathes in this place as the staff gets ready for this big open house and I can only imagine how Sloan is really feeling about seeing this through.

But she takes my hand and squeezes tightly. "Okay." No hesitation. A determined, sure answer. I like it. I like every word that's coming out of her mouth.

I smile and press my lips to her fingers locked in mine. "Okay."

When we're outside the playful Sloan returns. "I mean, it's for Abigail that I'm coming."

"Right, never thought it wasn't."

"I promised her *The Lion, the Witch, and the Wardrobe*. I'm not coming for you."

I knew that was the book she meant earlier, and feel a bit cocky that I did. "She'd be upset. I wouldn't care if you stayed here, obviously, I'm asking because of Abigail and her spelling words."

"Obviously."

I shudder. She said the word against my ear, her breath on my skin. I stop walking and tug on her hand. "You can't do that."

"What," she says again, her lips brushing my ear now. "This?"

I wheel her around, my palm on her face. Sloan doesn't look surprised, more expectant. "Yes, or I might forget where I am and kiss you in front of everyone."

Her eyes glimmer in the fading sunlight. Her voice soft. "Maybe you should."

"Gladly."

I kiss her, sweet and raw, with underlying desire.

We pull apart, laughing, when someone on the porch offers a sexy whistle. Sloan slings her arm around my waist and rests her head against my shoulder as we walk. Inside the truck, she slides across the front bench, our knees knocking together, her hand on my leg, and I don't remember when I've ever loved sitting in my truck more than this moment.

Chapter 13

Sloan

Saturday morning I let myself sleep into until seven thirty.

My mom tells me I'm one of those lunatics who loves to rise well before the sun, and it's true. I'm usually up before six. But last night we stayed up much too late, after promising Abigail we'd read some of the book when she got home from the birthday party. I might've rubbed it in Rowan's face when Abigail reported that the jewelry kit was the favorite and instead of playing a planned game the kids made bracelets.

Stretching my arms over my head, I grin, remembering those moments after Abigail went to bed. Moments by the fire, with strong arms around me. I forgot how good it felt to be held by a man. Even though Luke and I didn't break up that long ago, it's not like we spent our nights cuddling before that. I missed the signs, but we had drifted apart long before I caught him with Kayla, the recruiting manager.

Even thinking of them, my smile stays. I guess it's different being held by a man who cares. Being apart for these years can't erase the fact I've known Rowan Graham since he was seven. The way he kissed me gently, the way his hands left bursts of heat over my face, my arms, I hope it's the same for him.

I think that's why I feel comfortable with my abrupt plans today. I need to go to the lodge until noon to check off all the plumbing fixes, but after that, I have plans for Holly Berry Inn. No matter how much its big, burly owner might mutter and whine.

Wearing fuzzy socks that peek over the top of my boots and an oversized sweater, I have more Christmas spirit than I've had the entire season. I see Jeri first. She adjusts her coat and drifts toward the door.

"Hey girl," she says.

"Where are you going so early?" The sun is just peeking over the mountains.

"Oh, I'm actually off until Monday. Gifford is covering for me. You'll go nuts over his breakfast casserole. I think it's the chilis."

"Fun plans?"

"Yes," she says with a flush to her cheeks. "I'm meeting my cousin and apparently she's found my soul mate, according to her."

"I like the sound of that."

"Yeah, well—" Jeri tightens her grip on the duffle bag draped over her shoulder. "We'll see."

"Have fun."

I practically skip into the dining room. Abigail is still in her pajamas laughing with a tall guy with smooth, brown skin. He's drawing faces on her plate with ketchup. I take him for Gifford, the apron over his front giving him away. Rowan catches my eye and smiles over the rim of his mug. Liquid heat floods the bottom of my stomach with one look from the guy.

I've known him most of my life, true, but I've never known this feeling. Not around Rowan, honestly, not around anyone.

"Hi Sloan," Abigail says brightly.

"Hey cutie." I ruffle her hair and scoot against Rowan, without being too obvious. We haven't come out and said why, but we don't touch around Abigail. I think it's important to take that piece with a bit of care.

Rowan introduces me to Gifford who is ready and waiting with a plate of a sausage and egg casserole. Jeri wasn't lying, it's amazing.

Halfway through breakfast I slap my palms flat on the surface of the table. "So, here's the plan for today." Abigail jerks her head up, and Rowan looks nervous. "We are going to do something about the lack of Christmas trees in this old house."

"We get to pick one?"

"I told you we always get one," Rowan says. "I'm not that big of Scrooge that I'd let the kid go without a tree."

"How big are your trees here, Miss Abigail?" I ask.

"Shorter than me."

"Hey," Rowan says. "Are you throwing me under the bus?"

"Shameful, Rowan," I tell him, then look at Abigail. "Your uncle ought to be ashamed of himself. We are going to get a big tree!" I use my arms to talk, pleased when it draws out a squeal from Abigail. "And I'm going to bring the leftover decorations from the lodge and make the tree better than anything they've got at the North Pole!"

"Really!" Abigail jumps to her feet.

"Really," I say. "We've got the prettiest ornaments. What a shame it would be to just stuff them away until next year. Plus," I draw out the word, winking at Rowan. "I hear there is a special visitor at the park tonight."

Abigail shrieks. "We can go see Santa? Oh my gosh, can we get hot chocolates too? Nana and Pops always let me get hot chocolate, but last year we didn't get any because they didn't come."

I tsk at Rowan, shaking my head.

"I feel like you two ladies are ganging up on me," he says, stabbing his fork into my last piece of sausage and taking it for himself.

"We absolutely are, right Abs?" I say. "Girls gotta stick together."

"When can we go? Can we go now?"

"Take a chill, kid," Rowan says. "Sloan needs to go to work for a little while—"

"And get the decorations," Abigail says.

I shoot her with my fingers. "And the decorations. I'll make you a deal. Your uncle has a lot of work to do here, and if you help him out, then the faster we can leave once I get back. Can you help him out?"

"Yes," she says without a pause.

I grin at Rowan who watches me as if it is the first time he's seen me. Looking at me that way is more intimate than the kisses we've shared. It's strangely vulnerable. A look like that is something everyone deserves to experience at least once. I'd die happy if his eyes always burned like this, fierce and wanting.

Abigail hops off her chair and sprints toward the stairs to get dressed and ready. Rowan slips his fingers through mine under the table.

"You cheated. Making plans in front of Abigail, so I can't say no."

I laugh. "Be honest. You get the smallest tree that can still hold a present or two underneath it and probably put four ornaments on it."

"Five."

"And a wrapping bow as the star."

"Hey," he says. "Sometimes I make the bow myself. That takes some effort."

I kiss his cheek. "Not this year, mister. Your tree trimming belongs to me." I add a wicked laugh for good measure, and when he pulls me close, I'm too lost in him I almost miss my phone ringing on the table.

"Luke is calling," he says, his voice a little lower.

My shoulders slump. "Sorry," I say. The last thing I want to do is talk to Luke. "Give me a second."

I stand as I answer the phone, Luke is talking to someone else and doesn't seem to realize we're connected.

"Luke," I say sharply. "Luke."

"Oh, hey." He gives a final instruction to the person he's speaking with. "So, how did it go yesterday?"

"Fine," I say a little exasperated. "Luke, do I need to check in every day until the open house, or are you going to let me do this."

"Forgive me for wanting to make sure when Mark comes everything is in place."

I rub the bridge of my nose. I can feel Rowan watching me, but I don't turn around. "What do you need? I mean now—why did you call?"

"To see how it went, but also to let you know I made a reservation for us next Thursday at Paysha's. Your dad sounded pleased."

I am not going to dinner with Tracy, my dad, and Luke. That much I know, but I'm not going to argue with my ex in front of Rowan. "Hey, I need to get back up to the lodge."

"Why aren't you there?"

"I'm going to stay at the Holly Berry Inn," I say.

"What? Sloan, we only approved two nights for you."

"I'm covering the cost now."

He frees a grumbly sigh. "Why aren't you at the lodge? What a waste of time."

I peek over my shoulder shyly, watching Rowan clearing the table. "I found a few things that made Holly Berry more comfortable right now."

"Whatever," Luke says, distracted again by someone in the background. "I've got to go. We'll talk soon, and don't forget Thursday."

I hang up again without a goodbye and help Rowan walk the dishes into the kitchen.

"You're kind of short with your boss."

"How did you know he was my . . . oh, that's right, I forgot Sarah mentioned Luke yesterday."

He nods. "You don't like him?"

"You could say that." When I place my dishes in the sink, I bite the inside of my cheek. He ought to know, it's no big deal. Rowan and I always talked about relationships before. "Uh, he's my ex."

Rowan's eyes pop. "Didn't expect that. Were you serious?"

I hop onto the counter, hanging my legs off the edge. Rowan stands between my knees, on hand on either side of my hips. "Yeah. Three years." He lets out a breathy curse and I pinch his chest. "Hey, watch the mouth."

"Sorry," Rowan says with a grin. "That's a long time. I bet working with him isn't easy."

"It's not," I admit.

"Do you" – He clears his throat – "Do you have any feelings for him still?"

"Hmm, the whole curious jealous thing suits you," I say as I wrap my arms around his neck.

"I'm not jealous."

I pinch my finger and thumb together. "Maybe a little."

"Nope."

I grin against his lips and peck him quickly. "It hurt, I won't pretend it didn't, when I found out Luke was seeing someone behind my back. But I don't feel anything for him in that way. We shouldn't have been together as long as we were. I think it turned into more of a habit."

Rowan's eyes are steely. "He cheated on you?"

His voice is like the rumble of a storm. I sort of love it, but approach with caution. "Yeah."

Rowan kisses me. Hard. My fingers work up into his hair. His hands rest on my waist, holding me steady while his lips move as though they were made for mine. I'm breathless when he breaks away, his forehead on mine.

"He's the biggest idiot I've never met," Rowan says in a husky voice.

"Geez, if I'd known you'd go all feral mountain man on me, I would've opened with 'Hey long time no see, Rowan. By the way, my boyfriend was unfaithful' and let reuniting roll from there." He laughs and kisses my forehead. I trace the collar of his shirt, then his jaw. "What about you? Any ladies in town who will poison my food if they see me with you?"

"No," he says deliberately. "Not for a long time."

"Not sure I believe you."

"Believe it. A guy who owns an inn with a nine-year-old isn't something women line up for. My last relationship went south after I took guardianship of Abs."

I play with the scruff on the back of his neck, voice low. "I'm lining up. I didn't think you could get any better until . . . until I saw you again."

He nestles his face against my neck, kissing me there, then wraps his arms around me until I'm crushed against his chest. I don't mind.

"Sometimes I can't believe this is happening," he whispers. "I missed you, Sloan."

His forehead is on my shoulder, and I hold him there for a long time. I hate breaking this moment, being close to him, but if I want to spend a big chunk of the day back in these arms, I need to go. Reluctantly, Rowan backs away, reminded he also has a business to run. I kiss him quickly, and drive to the lodge feeling much the same as him: I can hardly believe this is happening.

Chapter 14

Rowan

Downtown reminds me of a town trapped inside a snow globe. Colorful lights wrap every tree in the park, and the different businesses have arranged decorative carts with different Christmas scenes. One looks like Santa's workshop with elves tangled in Christmas lights, another is a fireplace with a brother and sister trying to help a stuck Santa Claus up the chimney. Ice skaters, sledding, snowmen, every wintry scene is on display for people to ogle while they drink hot chocolate.

In the center is a red and green tent where families line up to visit the man of the hour. Sloan palms her hot chocolate, beaming while Abigail rattles off to the big guy on the throne. I don't know what she's telling him, but I like the way Sloan watches her like Abigail is the coolest kid in the world. Because she is.

"I love that she's still into this. My dad spilled the beans when I was six."

"What?" I whisper, careful not to ruin some random kid's Christmas. "By accident?"

She snorts and takes a sip of her drink. "No, he thought once I went to kindergarten I'd find out the truth anyway. My mom forbade me from telling any of the other kids on the playground, though."

"So what you're saying is you laughed at me behind my back until I was ten because I believed?"

She pats my cheek and grins. "But you were so cute about it."

I grunt. "Uncool, Sloan." I watch Abigail accept a pink and green candy cane from the woman dressed like an elf behind Santa Claus and march down the steps proudly. "I decided a while ago that I'm going to let Abs believe until she's twenty if she wants."

"I like that," she says and taps my elbow with hers.

Abigail runs up to us, taking my hand, then Sloan's, walking between us. She rambles on about all the things she's asking for this year. I remind her Santa Claus doesn't bring cell phones to anyone under the age of eighteen, then Sloan says sometimes he makes exceptions, but no younger than fourteen.

I like everything about the moment. As if my hard-built dynamic with Abigail went liquid to make room for one more piece in the shape of Sloan Hanson. I like watching Sloan and Abigail admire the carts with their scenes. I like watching how they try to help load the tree in the back of the truck. Back at the inn, watching Sloan hand Abigail fancy ornaments from the lodge boxes stirs something in my chest I didn't know existed. A feeling like my heart wants to break out of my chest, like I can't imagine a more perfect scene.

But the moment when I slip back inside the living room, well after ten o'clock and stumble onto Sloan softly reading from the chapter book, Abigail curled onto her lap, breathing softly, it's then I know I've never seen a more beautiful sight.

Leaning over the back of the couch, I wrap my arm around Sloan's shoulders and press a kiss to the joint of her jaw. I brush Abigail's hair off her forehead as Sloan closes the book, and rubs my arm around her chest.

"We made it two chapters before she gave in," she whispers.

I sneak around and scoop Abigail up from the couch. "Give me a second."

Abigail hardly moves when I place her in her bed and slip out of her room. My phone rings as I go back into the living room. Sloan turns, and I consider not answering, but they'll just call back.

"Hey mom," I say quietly. "Sorry, Abs crashed on you guys tonight."

"Oh, I thought so," my mom says, smiling back at me through the video. "We went to a movie and figured she'd probably be in bed."

I face the couch. Sloan bites her bottom lip, and fiddles with one of the pillows. I'd probably be weird around her parents too, but I want her to see them. Right now, I want everyone to know Sloan is back.

"Hey, want to say hi to someone?"

Sloan's eyes pop open and she seems ready to protest, but I flip the phone around too quickly, so she plasters a white smile on her face, hiding her nerves.

My mom squeals. "Sloanie! Devin, oh my gosh, get over here. It's Sloan."

"Hi, Loo," Sloan says, taking the phone from my hand. "It's been way too long."

"Sloan." My dad's voice joins. He sounds stronger. That's good. "Uh oh. Why are you and Rowan alone in the dark?"

"Oh, stop," my mom says. "It's called ambiance."

Sloan laughs and covers her face with one hand.

I peek over her shoulder. "Dad cool it, and Mom, it's called reading to your granddaughter by the Christmas tree."

"Right," my dad says.

"So, Sloan are you going to be up there for Christmas?" My mom claps her hands together, hoping. "We get in the day before Christmas Eve, oh I'd love to see you."

"Yeah." Sloan glances at me. "I will be around."

She digs into telling them about the work on the lodge and by the end of it all she's invited my parents to the open house. She's invited all of us.

"That sounds like a great time," my mom says. "A little different Christmas Eve than we're used to, but I bet Abby will go nuts for that cookie room you mentioned."

"It will be nice to have you there, that way I won't be tossed around with the hungry sharks who will be there to invest in the place," she tells them.

"Oh, Sloanie," my mom coos. "I'm so glad to see you, and to see you both together again. When Rowan was in his bad boy phase—"

"Oh, that's what we're calling it?" I interrupt.

"That's what I'm calling it," she goes on. "Anyway, there were a lot of nights I wished you'd somehow find him again and smack him. You were always good at putting him in his place."

Sloan laughs. "I would've, just for you, Loo."

The way she talks to my parents, it's as if no time has passed at all. But when the phone call ends, Sloan stares blankly at the new Christmas tree. She'd brought two themed boxes. One with red and green décor, the other with pale blue and white. She'd intended to let Abigail choose which color scheme, but the kid picked both. Still, I think it looks perfect.

I walk around the corner of the couch, my fingers going to her hair and brushing against the warmth of her neck. "What's up?" I sit next to her and without urging she nestles into my side.

"Your family is coming," she whispers is a sad voice.

"If you don't—"

"No," she says abruptly, her hand running over my chest. "I want them there. I want you there. I'm frustrated, is all."

"About what?"

"It took one invitation for your parents to come. One. After not seeing me for years. I just wish I could say the same for my side."

"Did you call your mom?"

"I need to."

I draw her in tighter against my side. "Tell her. Who cares what your dad thinks. He's not going to confront her there anyway, and if he does after, well it'd be done and you had your mom."

"So logical," she teases.

I smile and rest my cheek on the top of her head. "Your mom shouldn't be alone at Christmas because your dad has an issue. Besides, he's an investor, one of how many? This is your deal, not his."

"Ah, tell that to Tracy. She basically described me as Frankenstein's Monster, like my dad created me."

"No," I say, curling my arms around her and pressing a kiss to her forehead. "That stubborn determination, that's all you. Now, the rebellious side, I think that came because of your dad."

She laughs. "True. I do like making him red in the face." Sloan sighs and goes quiet for a long pause. "I wish we were close. Sometimes, when it was just me and him and no one to impress, we had fun. We both like card games and we'd play Blackjack, gambling over who picked dinner or something."

"He was nice to me," I admit. Shane Hanson wasn't the kind of dad who'd shoot hoops in the driveway or anything, but he'd taken us to water parks, and ice skating, and to the mall as kids. I never knew he had such a chip on his shoulder.

"Yeah. Things were better before he stepped out—I mean, obviously—but it's like the more his salary grew, the more he didn't care about breaking my mom's heart. Honestly, if she hadn't kicked him out finally, I could seriously see them being married right now, and Tracy just like the mistress with his kid."

"I felt bad for you with the divorce, but I'm kind of glad your mom doesn't need to put up with that anymore."

"Felt bad," she says, nudging me in the ribs. "Come on, we went and got milkshakes because I was relieved."

"I know, but I still felt bad."

Sloan lifts my hand and presses a kiss to my fingertips. My breath catches for half a second. I draw her in tightly.

"I could always count on you," she says softly. "You never let me down."

"Well, except for the big one, you know the whole not talking for—"

"Shh." She laughs and presses her fingers against my lips. "We'll forget that part for tonight. I'm trying to boost your ego. You were the one person I could always depend on."

"You still can," I say firmly. Curling one hand around the side of her face, I nudge her chin up, so she meets my eyes. "You can count on me, Sloan. I still want to be that for you."

There is a flicker of a smile in the corner of her mouth. She wraps her arm around my waist and rests her head back on my chest. We stay there, holding tightly to each other, until we both fall asleep.

For the couple of days the inn is a revolving door of skiers, people stopping in for a night, those coming for Christmas with family, some trying to get away from family. I'm glad when Jeri gets back, and glad Gifford stays to help with the demand.

Even with her sleeping at the inn, I feel as if Sloan and I rarely cross paths. She spends all day at the lodge and as the days creep nearer to the big event, I notice she chews on her thumbnail, and her knee bounces when she sits a lot. Abigail even noticed once and offered to share some of the lavender oil Sloan gave her, drawing out an easy laugh.

Four days before Christmas Eve she staggers in the door, exhausted but holding take-out containers from the Chinese place in town. "Jeri," she says. "I know your soulmate was a nightmare, so take a breather and come eat Chinese."

Jeri chuckles and gives her a lazy salute.

"Sloan," Abigail shouts, running down the stairs. "It was my last day of school today."

"I know," Sloan says, lifting the bags. "That's why we're celebrating with Chinese."

I go to her side and take some of the bags, leaning in closer. "And no one feels like cooking anything."

"Exactly," she says under her breath. "Hi, do I know you?"

I scoff as I set out the cartons. "I don't know, you sorta look familiar. It's been awhile since I've seen you though."

She plops into a seat next to Abigail and goes right for the chow mein. "I will be so glad to have this weekend over."

"Are you wishing away Christmas?" Jeri says as though she's offended.

Sloan chuckles. "Unfortunately, yes. Just this year though," she hurries to tell Abigail. "Next year, I promise to be the jolliest elf ever."

Next year. I crack a few knuckles before taking a seat next to Jeri on the opposite side of the table. My stomach jumps. Next year, and hopefully the year after that, and many more. With Sloan back in my life, I don't want to imagine it without her again. But her time here was never meant to be permanent, right? She had a job to do, and if she hadn't slammed into me again, she'd be leaving this weekend. Back home, to her life. Without me.

I pick at a piece of chicken, but look up when Sloan kicks my foot underneath the table. She tilts her head as if to ask, *What's up*? I flash her a smile, then go back to half-listening to Jeri rehash the weirdness of the blind date her cousin set her up with.

We haven't talked about what happens when Christmas is done. Where do we go? I know she lives about two hours south, but she's hinted she only stayed there for this project. What happens when the resort is open, and Sloan's job is done?

I watch her open fortune cookies with Abigail, laughing and trying again until they get what they want to hear. A smile teases my mouth. Doesn't matter where she is. I'm not saying goodbye to her again.

Not a chance.

Chapter 15

Sloan

"Rowan!" I feel like I'm ten again, plodding down the stairs, desperate to share something exciting. "Rowan!"

I dart through the front lobby, startling Abigail from her jigsaw puzzle, and weave through the crowds of guests keeping Jeri and Gifford running during breakfast this morning. I make a quick note to help with the clean up after I find the evasive owner of the inn. I shove through the back door, hardly caring that I'm in flats and not boots. Rowan stands by the four-wheeler, adjusting something on the handle. Keeping my legs lifted like a grasshopper, I pounce through the snow and fling my arms around his neck, taking him by surprise.

"Whoa," he says, but falls into my embrace and holds me close. "Sloan come on. You're in slippers."

"Flats, Rowan. Flats. Guess what! My mom is coming."

I love how he genuinely smiles. Luke would've brushed it off as nothing to freak out about, but Rowan's eyes brighten like he's as giddy as me.

"You got her to come? That's awesome. Where is she staying? Tell her to come here, we'll . . . we'll find her a room."

I don't care who sees for half a second and trap his face in my hands, then kiss him slowly, eagerly. A satisfied rumble comes from his throat and he kisses me back. Our cheeks are wet from the soft snowflakes falling once we break apart. I brush my hand on the side of his face. "Thank you," I whisper. "I'd have rolled over like I always do if it weren't for you. And so would she, but you don't have any open rooms, so I thought she could bunk with me. If that's okay."

"More than okay. I'll just charge you double."

I laugh and pinch his chest. "Sorry, I kissed you. I don't think anyone saw."

He stiffens, only slightly, and glances to the window as if he might see Abigail. "I'm not sure it matters."

My throat tightens. "It might be confusing."

"It might."

"I want to make sure we don't rush her."

"I want you."

At that, I freeze. His eyes are dark, beautiful, and simmering. His jaw is tight. Rowan reels me in, pulling on my arm until my body is pressed against his, chest to toes.

"Sloan," he says, voice rough. "I want you."

"This feels familiar," I say in a weird rush of panic.

"I hope it ends differently."

"You want Abigail to know about . . . this?"

He considers me, those eyes breaking through me until I feel as though my knees my give out.

"We can be slow with her, but I think she's already noticing things. And she likes you. Probably more than she likes me."

I snicker, fingers tracing the line of his mouth. "I doubt that."

Moments from the last week take my head in a spin. How quickly everything has changed. A man I have always wanted, needed, loved, is holding me saying the same. I want him. I want Abigail. I want this—all of it.

But my life a week ago didn't have them.

My life next week is not supposed to have them. So many fine details I haven't thought of, or perhaps, refused to let reality ruin these moments. Rowan curls my head against his shoulder. I breathe him in, the sweet woodsy scent of his skin, the perfect roughness of his hands, the softness of his voice.

"We'll figure it out," he says.

The vibration of his voice against my face brings a warm calm. "How did you know I was thinking things?"

His fingers stroke the ends of my hair. "Because I know you, the same as you know me. We'll figure it out."

Okay. I don't say it out loud, but I close my eyes, feet freezing. Imagining a life where I am not standing here, in this moment, isn't worth imagining. I don't want to be anywhere else but right here in the arms of Rowan Graham.

I finish everything on my list before lunch is cleared away. Today I was able to do everything at the inn, and I'm glad. Staying at Holly Berry is feeling more like home than anywhere. Jeri is out with her family who is gathering in town for the holidays. So it's just Abigail, me, and Rowan around the table trying to finish up the last of the puzzle when Rowan's phone rings.

I notice the shadow that crosses his face, but Abigail is gleefully oblivious. He flashes me a glance before standing all at once and disappearing into the other room to take the call. I swallow past a knot. Something is up.

"I can't wait for your party," Abigail says. "Will Santa Claus be there?"

"No. He's going to be pretty busy on Christmas Eve delivering presents to naughty kids like you."

She giggles when I try to tickle the spot between her shoulder and neck. "Good kids."

"Oh, right," I say as I slip a piece of her puzzle in place. "You have been good. Shoot, I better fix the letter I sent him."

She laughs again and calls me weird at the same time Rowan comes back into the room. His face is like a stone. I see the small muscles in his jaw flinch when he places a hand on Abigail's shoulder. I try to catch his eye, but he's not looking at me, and I think it's intentional.

"Hey kid," he says in a low tremble. "Guess who else wanted to stop in and see you this Christmas?"

Abigail tilts her head. "Who?"

"Uh, your dad is in town."

My stomach drops out the bottoms of my shoes. Rowan is fighting to keep his voice light, and fighting even harder to draw the smallest grin for Abigail's sake.

A deep furrow builds in the center of her forehead. "Dad? He's here?"

"Uh, yeah. I guess he had work in Denver, and decided to stop by without telling anyone before he left." There's annoyance in his voice, truth told, there is downright bitterness, but he keeps that stern grin. "Great right."

Abigail seems conflicted. "When is he coming?"

"Well, right now. He wanted to take you out. Just you and him, for a treat or something, but it's up to you if you want to go."

She looks up at her uncle. "What do you think?"

Maybe Abigail doesn't catch the way Rowan wants to protest, but I do. His distaste for this idea is written in his stiff movements, the tension in his face. "It's up to you, kiddo. Really. We can stay here, or you can go on a quick date. Up to you."

Her breaths start to come quicker. I reach out and squeeze her hand, building pressure that is grounding. "Abby," I say softly. "There isn't a wrong answer. No one is going to get their feelings hurt."

"I don't want to leave you guys out," she admits.

"We won't be left out," Rowan assures. "And neither will your dad if you want to stay here."

It takes another minute, but eventually Abigail nods and says, "Well, maybe I should go with him. He's never here."

Rowan ruffles her hair. "Okay, kid. Go get your shoes on then."

She doesn't rush off, but slowly saunters up the steps as if deep in thought. I bite the inside of my cheek when I take Rowan's hand. "You good?"

He shakes his head. "Scott is . . . he's something else. He's been here for five days and didn't think to call me?"

There's more. Rowan seems ready to punch a hole in the wall. "What's going on?"

His eyes flash with angry heat. "He told me he has a house, that he's doing really well out there."

"Anything else?" I don't know if I want to know.

"It's pretty clear what he's alluding to." Rowan slumps into the chair and rakes his fingers through his thick hair. "Temporary, I knew I was signing up for temporary guardianship, but now . . ."

"You don't want her to go."

He shakes his head. “I don’t. Scott doesn’t know anything about her. He’s kept himself away. Why now?” His voice is desperate. “Why stroll back in and just because he has a house, he’s all for it. He doesn’t know her.”

I lace my fingers with his, not knowing what to say. I don’t want Abigail to go, but the man is her father. “Talk to him,” is all I can come up with. “Just . . . talk with him. I wish this wasn’t happening.”

“Yeah,” he mutters, but puts a grin on when Abigail’s steps come back down the steps. “Ready to go?”

“Ready,” she says mildly.

The front doors open not ten minutes later. I stand out of the way, not sure where my place is in all this, and watch from the safety of the corner as a man in a nice business coat brushes his feet on the rug. When he peels off his sunglasses, I recognize him. A little older, with the faintest hint of lines by his eyes, but he’s the guy I remember hanging around with Jenny when I was still wearing braces.

“Scott,” Rowan says, voice low and raw.

Scott spins around, an unsteady smile on his face as he holds out a hand for Rowan. “Hey,” he says, his eyes drifting to Abigail who clings to Rowan’s arm. She wants to stand tall, I can see it in the way she keeps rolling her shoulders back, but the poor girl is so torn and I hate it.

Rowan shakes Scott’s hand, then urges Abigail forward as Scott crouches so he can meet her eyes.

"Hi sweetheart," Scott says, brushing a knuckle over her cheek. "You got big."

"Yeah."

"It's good to see you." He sounds sincere; there is a tremble in his voice.

Rowan's face is pale, and I want to stop the ache that's, doubtless, peeling back the layers of his heart as he watches this unfold. What a position to be in. Wanting the best for your niece, raising her, but knowing one day it might end. To know maybe that day is now.

"Hey, Abby," Scott says. "Do you mind if I talk with your uncle first, then we'll go get hot chocolate, and maybe we can go ice skating. You still like that, right?"

She nods vigorously, smiling a little wider. He smiles too, and taps her nose before standing again.

"Can we talk, Rowan?"

I close my eyes and hug my middle. Why is he doing this right before Christmas? Why do I feel like I have a say in this family, in Abigail, or her father? I cross the room and take Abigail's hand. "We'll finish this puzzle while we wait."

Scott looks at me like he might recognize me, but doesn't ask. Rowan opens his arm and ushers Scott to the back office. He spares a preoccupied glance my way, and I smile. All I can do is hope he knows I'm here when this is all over, and whatever is going to happen, I'll always be here.

Chapter 16

Rowan

Scott looks at the family pictures on the shelf for a long time. He reaches out and touches a picture of Jenny the day Abigail was born.

My stomach sinks. He hurts, but I still hold resentment. This guy never showed my sister how much she mattered, and he lost his chance. I don't want to give him a chance to make amends with Abigail, and I feel a little like a beast for it. Abigail deserves her parents, and if she can't have her mom, shouldn't her dad be the one to be in her life?

I sit behind my desk, wanting to get his over with, wanting to drag it out as long as I can.

Scott takes a picture of Abigail when she turned five in his hands and laughs. "You've been so good to her, Rowan."

"Want coffee, or water, or anything?"

He returns the picture and takes a deep breath. "Uh, no. I'm good. Listen, I know what you must be thinking."

"I don't know if you do."

He takes the chair on the opposite side of the desk. "I didn't call you about being in town for a reason. I wanted, well, I wanted to think before we met."

"About what?"

Scott leans back in the chair, crosses his arms over his chest. "I'm not a good dad, Rowan. I know that."

Not what I expected to come out of his mouth, but I don't disagree. I don't say anything.

"I wasn't that great of a husband to be honest, and I'm ashamed to say it's taken me this long to see it. I loved Jenny; I did. The best I knew how. I was faithful to her, and just . . . when she got sick, I—it's like I pushed her away to avoid the pain that I knew was coming. Trust me, Rowan, if I could go back . . ."

I rub the back of my neck. Everything he's saying I understand too well. The agony of losing someone you love, sometimes it's simpler to shut off. Hadn't I done that when Jen died, except I shoved Sloan away. Not until Abigail came to us did I start opening up again.

"It's no excuse," Scott goes on, his voice hoarse. "But it's how I handled it. With Abby, I was angry. So often. I saw how I was hurting her, but I didn't know how to be the person she'd need. I was distant, and I know I neglected her. I will never be able to express to your mom and dad, to you, what it means that you took her and filled the pieces I just couldn't fill."

"Scott, listen—"

"No, please." He holds up a hand. "I'm not saying this for any sympathy or forgiveness, I'm not sure I deserve it. Not yet. But it did get me thinking, unselfishly, for maybe the first time since Jenny died." He leans over his knees and studies his hands. "Things are going well. I got a decent promotion."

"You feel you're ready for Abigail." Not a question. The words come out in a kind of somber declaration.

Scott looks up, his eyes are glassy. "With my job—" He clears his throat. Is he . . . getting emotional? "With the new position I'm going to be on the road, in the air, I'm going all over training different branches of the call center. I'm talking Brazil, Philippines, Japan, India. Maybe Alabama for the fun of it."

I can't help but give a little laugh when he does.

He smiles and stares at his hands again, his smile fading. "I want to be a good piece of Abigail's life, Rowan. I want what is best for her, and for there to be constants that she can count on while she grows up. I-I love her, truly."

"I know, Scott. She's impossible not to love."

He wipes his eyes with the heel of one hand and clears his throat again. "As I said, I want a constant for her. I want to . . . I want to see what you think of . . . taking permanent guardianship. Please, don't judge me for this Rowan, it's not that I don't want her, because I *wish* I were a better father, I do. This is the one thing I feel I can do for Abigail that gives her stability."

I can't breathe. Scott and I stare at each other for at least a minute before he taps the desk.

"Say something, please."

"Permanent guardianship?" She'd be mine. For good.

He nods and wipes his eyes again. "If you're willing. I'm going to be gone a lot, and she needs someone who can make choices about her health, and school, and . . . all of it."

"I'm willing," I blurt out before he can change his mind.

His face twists in a grimace and I remind myself to be sensitive. As poor of a role model as Scott has been, clearly, he loves Abigail.

"I still want to be in her life though," he says. "Please, let me be there as another dad figure, but you . . . you're more her father than I've ever been. I won't step on your toes; you know her and I have full confidence that you'll do what's best for her. But like birthdays, holidays, I'd like to see her, you know, and do things like we're going to do today."

"She'd love that," I say sincerely. This way she can just have a relationship with him without the bad stuff. They can just love each other and live their lives. I'll be the one she can complain to him about—when her dad—*me*—is being unreasonable. But I'll be the one she'll cry to when someone breaks her heart. I'll get those moments.

Scott blows out a long breath. "Do you think she'll hate me?"

I shake my head, hoping I'm right. "Not if you're around, Scott. When she's old enough, I think she'll see that you love her and wanted what was best for her. We all want what is best for her."

He sniffs and stands, pulling out an envelope from the pocket of his coat. "I'll never be able to repay you for this, Rowan. Here are some documents we'll need to file with the courts."

I touch the envelope gingerly.

"I'm going to talk with her today," he tells me. "Try to explain. Don't worry I've been practicing, and won't dump too much heavy stuff on her. I just want her to know I love her. I'm going to promise not to miss a birthday, though, so you better take a reservation for me in January. I'll be back."

I laugh and do something I don't think I've done with Scott Lund since his wedding day. Hug him. We both clap each other on the back, both crying like idiots, and take a moment to compose ourselves before stepping out of the office.

"Abs," he says brightly. "Ready for ice skating!"

"Ready!" she squeals and hops up from the chair.

Scott glances over his shoulder at me and smiles, then disappears into the fading afternoon, Abigail already jabbering on about the difference between roller blading and ice skating.

I startle when Sloan wraps her arms around my waist. I pull her close, and press a kiss to the top of her head, breathing her sweetness in.

"What happened?" Her voice quivers.

"She's mine," I whisper against her head. My arms are trembling as I hold her, still unsure if what just happened is real.

Sloan looks at me, tears in her eyes. "Seriously?"

I nod and kiss her. Feeling her against me is all I want to do right now. I'll fill her in on all the details later.

"Abs, you're getting your slobber all over the window," I say.

She snorts, but keeps her face pressed against the front window. "I want to see them when they pull up. Where is Sloan again?"

"Probably right behind them. She just went to pick up her mom at the airport."

Abigail smashes her nose to the glass, dressed in her new snow hat, new gloves, and squeezing a stuffed bunny with ice skates. Scott wanted to watch her open her Christmas presents before he left, and she hasn't put them down since. He did a decent job explaining things, did promise to not miss a birthday, and left his daughter with the gummiest grin I've seen on her face for a long time.

All day I keep steeling glances at her, hardly believing that she's mine. No awkward petitions in January like I'd planned; she knows who has her back while she grows up. It was always this unknown hanging over us. Abigail understood she might leave someday, but now—this morning looked a whole lot different.

"Oh, oh, there they are."

Outside Sloan's rental SUV pulls up, and not far behind another truck follows closely. Every year, my dad insists he have his own car to do whatever he wants. But with his lungs, he doesn't do much but hang out at the inn. It's easier to give into a few things. Abigail laughs when we hear squeals out in the parking lot. I hold open the door and watch as Sloan's mom runs to mine, hugging and laughing, like long lost friends. But in a way they kind of are too.

"Nana! Pops!" Abigail shouts and darts into the snowy lot. My mom turns from Kristine and swallows Abigail up.

"Rowan, oh my goodness, look at you." Kristine tugs me into the mix and hugs me. Sloan tries to muffle her laugh. Her mom is five foot even, so I practically bend in half to let her squeeze my neck. "You're huge, kid."

"It's good to see you," I say. "It's been a long time."

She pulls back, smiling. "Too long. Thanks for letting Sloan squat with you, then again it sounds like you haven't minded."

She pats my face that feels as though my skin lights on fire.

"Mom," Sloan says with a groan as she takes Kristine's arm. "You promised."

"What? I didn't say anything."

I scratch the back of my neck before herding the new group inside. We gather around one of the tables, eat leftover cinnamon rolls from breakfast, laughing and catching up with the last eight years. A rush fills my chest, when Kristine hands Abigail a wrapped present to put under the tree next to the piles my parents brought.

"She bought Abigail a gift?" I whisper to Sloan.

She shrugs. "I mentioned her, and the all-children-must-be-spoiled side of Kristine Hanson took over."

I smile. "That's . . . awesome."

The afternoon is spent playing card games, letting Abigail eat too much sugar, me lazily doing a few things since I do run an inn. A few guests scuttle in and out, but I think my mom enjoys greeting people since every time the bells on the doors ding, she hops up and guides them to where they want to go or offers Jeri's cookies, and if she lived closer I think I'd hire her. She has a knack for getting complete strangers laughing.

"We ought to get some takeout," my dad says once the sun is long gone. He nudges Abigail's shoulder, trying not to appear too tired. "Pizza?"

"Pizza," she agrees.

Sloan stands. "I need to make a call and cancel something; I'll be just a second."

Kristine frowns and when Sloan is gone, I tap her shoulder. "What's with that face?"

"Sorry, I don't hide feelings well, I guess." She juts her chin at the door. "She's canceling a dinner. Her dad wants her to join him and dumb Luke tonight. I tell you what, Rowan, that man." She shakes her head and takes a soothing drink of her tea. "Shane would shove Luke in Sloan's face until the end of time since he thinks he's the guy she ought to be with. No mind that he's a dirtbag."

My jaw tightens and I slump against the couch. "She doesn't deserve that."

"No, she doesn't," Kristine agrees and pats my knee. "I'm glad she ran into you. I think you reminded her of that too."

I scoff. "Sloan never had a problem telling guys they weren't worthy of her. And she said that, *you're not worthy of me*."

We laugh together. More than Pizza Ian, guys who stepped on Sloan's toes knew their mistake quickly. It makes knowing the sort of struggles, with pleasing and being enough, she kept inside harder to understand.

"But she had you back then too."

"I don't think I had much to do with it."

"Ah, but you always had her back. That gives a bit of confidence to anyone, knowing someone will be there if you fall on your face." Kristine sighs and studies her tea. "It took her a long time to kick Luke to the curb, longer than it should've if you're asking me, and even if you aren't, I'm telling you. I was the only one who praised her for it. Everyone else, well, they made it seem like she was a fool for not looking the other way and just dealing with his shenanigans."

I don't like that, not at all. Maybe going to the lodge with all these people isn't such a good idea. But when Sloan strolls back in, a smile on her face, I change my mind. I think I'd follow her anywhere.

She settles at my side and takes up her own cup again. "I'm ready for pizza."

"Everything good?" I ask.

She grins with a nod. "Yep. I'm exactly where I want to be tonight."

Chapter 17

Sloan

"We are having a girls' lunch," Loo declares after breakfast is just barely cleared away on Christmas Eve. "It has been too long since I've seen you and your mom and I need some gossip in my life. Devin won't indulge me."

I chuckle as I finish the French braid in Abigail's hair. Just for fun. "I am all for it."

"Fine," Rowan grumbles. "Then we're taking this twerp sledding, right Dad?"

Devin nods and Abigail darts away to get her snow clothes.

"Jeri," I say, peeking my head into the kitchen. "Come with us. We're going out for lunch."

Jeri whoops and closes the refrigerator with more energy than before. "I look a sight—"

"Stop," I say as I thread my arm through hers. "You are perfect, and there isn't any need to get all glammed up when we're going to be shoveling buckets of fried food and molten chocolate cake in our mouths anyway."

She moans. "Yes, please."

We all squeeze into the SUV and drive into town. I don't remember the last time I spent a full afternoon with my mom. I've been too tied up in the lodge, but with Loo and Jeri added to the mix makes this all the better. We take a scenic route and show Jeri where Rowan grew up since she insists he's never told her, then we point to the house around the corner where I lived. There is an alleyway that gives access to a water well that connected our fences, and now I'm able to confess to the many nights Rowan and I snuck out to cause trouble with our friends.

At the diner we crowd around a booth, hardly speaking to each other since locals in for a holiday lunch gab with Jeri, or my mom, and Loo about old times. It's as if we never left and are still part of the town.

"So, Sloan," Loo says. "Tell us what to expect tonight. How do we act?"

"Like yourselves," I say with a little laugh.

"Well, it's a valid question, what with all the fancy folks coming."

"Loo," I say, "the open house is for everyone. There will be a lot of people from town visiting along with buyers and investors. My goal has always been to make the lodge homey and comfortable, for anyone. I guess tonight will be the first test if I got it right."

Mom squeezes my shoulders. "It's going to be perfect, sweets."

"I wish I could go," Jeri pouts.

"Oh, but you'll have fun with your family. Didn't you say grandma is quite a cook, too?"

She nods, a little color tinting her cheeks. One thing I've learned about Jericho is she doesn't care to be put on a pedestal about her cooking or the legacy she comes from. "Yeah, we all know our way around a kitchen."

"Maybe if the party is boring we'll slip over to your house and eat. I bet it's quite a spread," I tell her.

She laughs and goes into how her parents can never decide what the main course will be when it comes to big family dinners. Without fail every holiday any cultural cuisine that can be imagined usually graces their table in some way.

"Linguini next to tacos?" Loo says. "Sounds like my sort of dinner."

"Well, as fun as seeing the fam will be, I'd kill to see Rowan get all fancy in a suit. I can hardly imagine him without his boots and coat," Jeri says.

I grin shyly, not willing to admit I've thought of little else than what Rowan will look like tonight. He's delicious as he is, but I have no doubts the man cleans up brilliantly.

"I've not seen him smile as much as I have in the twenty-four hours we've been here in forever," Loo says with a touch of mischief as she sips her lemon water. She's peeking at me over the rim of her glass.

"Oh, I agree," Jeri adds. "He's a regular holly jolly this year."

She winks at me.

"Well obviously," I say. "The inn has been maxed out for nearly two weeks. He's bringing in the big bucks. I'd be smiling too."

Loo pats my shoulder and snickers. "Oh, you're so cute how you're trying to take the attention off you."

My cheeks burn, but I can't keep my smile under wraps. "I'm glad we ran into each other again too. Happy?"

"Very," Mom says, and Loo nods.

"Sloanie, you don't see what you did for my son, do you? Even now." Loo slowly shifts bits of lettuce around on her plate. "You two had something so unique, especially for a boy and girl. When you moved away, I saw a hole in his heart the same size as the one he had for Jenny."

My smile disappears and an unwelcome sting builds behind my eyes. Even being together now, the pain of our years apart is still a raw, open wound that needs to close. I hope the more Rowan is in my life the smaller the hole will grow.

"Then," Loo goes on, "those years when he just didn't know what path he wanted to take, I could see him trying so hard to compensate for missing you."

"Me?"

Jeri taps the table, and talks through a bite of her halibut. "Are these the Laura years?"

Loo nods, her lips tight.

"Laura years?" I ask. Rowan mentioned an old relationship, but we've been too wrapped up in being together again we haven't even spoken much about Luke or Rowan's old girlfriends.

"Laura was a girl he met when he was in Texas," Loo says. "She had her own demons to conquer, but she wasn't who Rowan needed. She fed his anger and hurt instead of supporting him."

"I don't understand?"

Loo huffs and sinks into the booth a little. "She knew he hurt. He'd tell her things, then she'd use them against him. Like threatening to leave him if he didn't do as she pleased since losing Jenny and losing you left that boy afraid to lose anyone really. Even through his wildness he called us every other day at least. I think it was a way to know he wasn't alone. And with Abigail, he'd Skype with her every Sunday, even before she could really talk."

I press a palm to my chest; an ache comes from the truth and I wish I could go back and be there for Rowan. He wishes he tried harder, but I should've tried harder too. I knew how to get in touch with Loo and Devin, I could've called him the same as he could've called me.

"What happened with Laura?"

Loo grimaces. "She kept him numb with drinks, and he kept her satisfied by funding her lifestyle. You know, he thought he'd marry her. I don't think it's because he loved her, not really, more that he didn't know how to walk away. Things got worse between them when Rowan started to clean up his act, started taking college seriously, and stopped living the night life. She was pretty cruel to him."

"Cruel?" I have a sudden desire to meet this Laura, and not for friendly reasons.

"You know, she'd degrade him. Tell him he wasn't a real man, or try to make him jealous by meeting other guys at bars and parties."

"And he didn't break up with her?"

Loo shakes her head. "I didn't think he'd ever cut ties, until Scott asked us to take Abigail. Rowan jumped in without a second thought, but Laura wasn't exactly warm to the idea of taking on a kid and him not reenlisting."

"Ugh." Jeri winces as if she ate something sour. "This is the famous ultimatum, right?"

"How do you know so much?" I ask with a pinch to her arm.

"Have you not noticed that I have a talent of getting people to confess everything to me?"

My mom and I laugh, but Loo crosses her arms over her chest with a frown. "Laura thought she'd be clever and give Rowan an ultimatum to choose her or his niece." She chuckles bitterly. "He didn't even hesitate and came home for Abigail."

I swipe a tear from my cheek, a little embarrassed I'm crying, but Loo simply squeezes my hand.

Jeri nudges my shoulder. "The point is, I'm glad you showed up on our doorstep."

"Me too," Loo says. "Something about you brings out the real Rowan. Always has."

My mom grins at me, then glances at Loo. "Well, as her mom, I think the same could be said about that giant of a man. Seriously, when did he get so tall?"

I laugh and wipe my eyes. "You guys need to stop, or we need to get back to the inn."

"Why?" Loo asks.

I scoff. "I'm not sure his mother would like to hear how badly I want to kiss him right now."

Loo squeezes my hand again and says, "When it's coming from your mouth, Sloan, I don't mind hearing any of that gushy stuff. Not at all."

We talk of brighter things the rest of the meal. Things like my mom's cake business, and Loo and Devin's unique neighbors in Nevada. When Jeri tells us she needs to hit the road, we drive back to the inn, belting out Christmas songs, laughing like maniacs.

A few snow sleds are leaning against the side of the house, and when my mom and Loo are properly distracted by Abigail's retelling of the morning on the hills, I sneak away to find a certain innkeeper. He's in his office, and I'm mightily glad there is a door I can close behind for a touch of privacy.

"Hey," he says at the sound of the door shutting. "You're back."

I am across the room and behind his desk before he finishes. The way his eyes widen in surprise as I take his face between my palms sends my heart flipping in my chest. I kiss him, good and thorough. Rowan frees a soft groan and tugs me onto his lap, his arms holding me steady as I kiss him and kiss him and kiss him.

"What was that?" he whispers against my mouth when I pull back.

"You are wonderful, have I told you?"

"I don't know where this is coming from, but I like it."

"I should've been there with you all this time, Rowan," I say, pressing my cheek against his.

"Sloan—"

"No, it's okay. We can't change it, but I think you're wonderful, and I would've never given you an ultimatum. I would've been there; I would've picked you up. I *wish* I could've picked you up." I draw in a shuddering breath.

His arms tighten around my waist and he buries his face into my shoulder. "My mom has been gossiping."

I only nod, afraid my voice will break again.

He chuckles, but it's a sad sound. "I wanted to forget . . . you." Rowan pulls back, his rough hand on my cheek. "Turns out you're far too memorable."

"Obviously." I laugh weirdly, sort of cross between a giggle and sob, then kiss him, and I don't stop until we need to come up for a little bit of air.

"You look so pretty, sweetie," my mom says when she steps out of the bathroom.

"Dang, mom." I scan the black dress hugging her figure with just the right amount of sparkle to the fabric. "When did you get that dress?"

She snorts and a red flush tints the bridge of her cheeks. "Oh, a little while ago."

"Don't let Dad see you, no, scratch that—do let him see you. He needs to see what he gave up."

"Sloan," she says, but she's smiling. "I thought you two were getting along better."

"We're fine when it's just us. But put him in public with a crowd to impress—" I shake my head. "It's fine."

"He's not going to be thrilled I came."

"Yeah, but he already brought Hallie, so he won't keep her away, and he won't cause any drama because that would look bad on him. It's better to ambush the man."

My mom laughs and hands me a silver bracelet that matches my royal blue dress. "I'm so glad I came. I can't wait to see all your hard work. Tonight will be wonderful, but you, my girl, need to breathe. You're like a drum, wound up all tight."

I blow out a long breath, adding another splash of color to my lips. "It's going to be great." I'm not saying it for her, I'm saying it for me.

Downstairs Rowan and his family are gathered and waiting. He faces me, and I nearly stumble off the last step. My eyes bug out, and my throat is drier than the summer. A suit on Rowan Graham. Yes, please. His broad shoulders fit perfectly, he's trimmed his beard, and I don't even try to stop my eyes from roving over his body.

"Wow, Sloan," he says, drawing me back to the moment. "You look beautiful."

"Thanks." My voice is all wrong and husky. "You are too. You look sexy —I mean, good. Abigail, don't repeat that."

The girl snickers and takes her coat from her grandpa. Rowan takes my hand, and lets my mom loop her arm through his other arm as we step into the cold, waving to Sam, a fill-in to keep watch over the inn while we're out.

Driving in a nice dress is awkward, but I don't know how long I'll need to stay, so taking separate cars seems the obvious idea. When we pull up the lane, Moosehead Lodge is bright, the wide porch is decked in Christmas lights and fresh, pine bough wreaths. I love the carved bear sculptures at the doorway, ready to greet guests. The walkway is lined in a lighted railing, every curve reminds me of a trail leading into a fairy land. Mom's mouth drops as she studies the breadth of the building. She doesn't say anything, simply squeezes my arm and beams.

Coat attendants are there to take items and Rowan stares at the man suspiciously as he takes his coat and his mom's purse.

"They'll be locked up," I whisper.

"Oh, who cares, I've got nothing these people are going to want," Loo says as she reaches for a glass of spiced eggnog.

I lead them around the different rooms, showing off the sitting areas, the game loft. Devin and Rowan are distracted by the sports room where guests will be able to come for hunting season, snowboarding, skiing, even snowshoeing and ice-fishing tours.

"Sloan, there you are."

I close my eyes, my fingernails carve half-moons into my palms. My mom snorts after she looks behind us, and takes a long drink of her eggnog. Rowan had been laughing with his dad, but he must notice the steely shift in my countenance and slowly his grin fades.

Holding my breath, I turn around. "Hi, Luke."

He looks perfectly handsome in his fitted suit, and expensive haircut. Luke is grinning, but I've known the man long enough to know when he's faking it. He leans in and kisses my cheek. "Looks perfect. Would've been nice to see this dress last night instead of you canceling."

"I had important things to take care of," I say innocently.

His eyes flick to my mom, and he lifts a glass, an edge in his voice. "Kristine. Good of you to come."

"Luke," is all she says before turning to Loo and Devin.

I'd laugh if it weren't so terribly uncomfortable. The older two Grahams look like they want to bury Luke out back. I'm sure the gossip came from my mom. I doubt Rowan took the time to dig into my former love life with his parents. I am about to feel rather empowered until I see my father and Tracy.

"Sloan!" Ah, at least Hallie makes me smile. My little sister is a ball of sunshine that breaks the tension in two.

"Tiny, hi!" I squeeze her against me, blonde curls tickle under my nose. She is petite and short for her age, but I think she's starting to grow into herself. "You look so pretty. Have you seen the cookie room yet?"

Hallie shakes her head, then brightens when she sees my mom. "I didn't know you'd be here, Krissy!" She hugs my mom and my mom genuinely hugs her back.

"I couldn't miss your sister's big night."

"A surprise, Kristine," my dad says.

"Well, Shane, I figured it matters more if Sloan wants me here than you."

I shake out my hands, but relax when I feel a gentle touch on the small of my back. Rowan's dark eyes calm me in another heartbeat.

Luke claps his hands, and I suppose I can thank the man for recognizing a fight brewing. At least he stops it before it can explode. "Sloan, aren't you going to introduce us?"

"Uh, these are the Grahams. The best people I know, and long-time friends, and this is Luke Harrington, the Vice President of operations with the resort."

Loo offers a stiff nod, and Devin politely shakes his hand, but he's not smiling. Rowan stays by me and seems pleased when the conversation shifts before Luke gets to him.

"Devin," my dad says, and reaches out his hand. "Good to see you."

Devin is pleasant as ever (more than with Luke). His shoulders sag a bit, and his eyes droop, but he claps my dad on his shoulder and laughs like he's ready to run circles around the room.

"I didn't recognize you and Loo and—" Dad's eyes go to Rowan. "Rowan. You were nothing but a kid last time we saw each other."

Rowan is gracious and shakes my dad's hand. "Been a long time Mr. Hanson."

"He's cute," Hallie whispers into my ear.

"I know," I say and pinch her arm. "You've met him, you know. But you were just little."

"Really? You've been friends that long?" She winces when her lip gets caught in one of her braces' brackets. Tracy scolds her for picking her teeth, but Hallie still seems more interested in Rowan.

"We've known each other even longer than that. Since I was seven."

"Funny, you never mentioned him." Luke inserts himself into the conversation.

"Well," I say with a quick glance at Rowan before I turn quite gutsy and take his hand. "We sort of lost touch, and I certainly didn't expect to reconnect at the Holly Berry Inn."

Luke's face isn't pleased, and he wholly notices the way I'm touching this man. "Huh," he says. "Well, we need to do a few things. If you'll excuse us, I need to steal Sloan away."

Luke holds his arm out as though I might slip beside him and let him hold my waist or something. Instead, I tug on one of Hallie's curls and gesture for Abigail to come to us. "Hal, this is Abby. Since I'm sure you guys are going to be bored stiff with all the adult stuff, why don't you stick together and go to the cookie room."

"Oh, I'll take them," my mom offers.

Tracy frowns, but she simply lifts her chin and clings to my dad's arm tighter.

"Thank you," Hallie says dramatically. I can hear her questioning Abigail about her age, likes, and where she lives. They'll be fine.

"Sloan," Luke says impatiently.

I give Rowan a quick smile. "See you in a second."

"Go, do your thing. I'll keep my parents from embarrassing you."

Devin is still idly chatting with my dad. They were always nice about what happened between my parents, and truth told, my dad and Rowan's parents were friendly. I'm glad the low-key attitude of the Grahams is here to keep my dad's head from imploding with self-importance.

When we're out of earshot, Luke takes hold of my arm and leans close. "What are you doing, Sloan?" His voice is gravelly, threatening.

"Working." I shirk him off. "Now, tell me who I'm supposed to speak with, then I'd like to get back to my family."

Luke narrowed his eyes. "Who is that guy you were all over?"

"All over?" I roll my eyes. "Get a grip, Luke."

"No," he says. "You've been on company time and if you've been—"

"Stop it," I snap. "I know what you're about to accuse me of, and if you don't want me to slap you in the face, you'll shut your mouth. Rowan bought the inn years ago, and I didn't know. We were best friends when I lived here and simply reconnected."

"Clearly."

"Stop it. You don't get to pry into my life anymore. Now, come on. It's Christmas Eve and I refuse to argue with you on Christmas Eve."

After a moment his mouth twitches into a vicious sort of grin. "You're right. No need to fight. This way." He holds out his hand so I can go first. "Mark is over here and wants you to meet some of the first buyers."

A shiver runs down my spine. Luke wasn't ever the jealous type. Maybe because he was already cheating, but I don't like his possessiveness tonight. I don't like the way he accused me of being inappropriate professionally. Bottom line, I don't like the way Luke fakes his grin the entire time we talk with Mark Bridger and some of the wealthiest future residents.

He's got the same look a hunter has when they see the catch they're after and will do anything to get what they want.

Chapter 18

Rowan

It's a strange Christmas Eve. I'm used to quiet, not fancy drinks, and suits, and jewelry.

Abigail seems to be enjoying herself with Hallie, the two girls have frosted and decorated at least a dozen Christmas cookies with other kids in the cookie room. Kristine and my mom have snapped a thousand pictures, and I can see what Sloan means about her mom being a gem. Hallie poses for Kristine, laughing and giggling, and anyone looking in from the outside would never know the truth. Sometimes I wonder what will happen when Hallie is old enough to figure it out. It's not something that won't be obvious. I like to think Hallie will love Kristine all the more for it.

"It's quite a surprise seeing you after all this time."

I turn to Shane standing behind me, a glass in one hand, his other tucked into his slacks. I don't know where my dad is, or Shane's wife.

As if he knows who I'm scanning the room for, Shane steps to my side. "Tracy is showing off the brickwork to your dad, and he's being polite and appeasing her."

I chuckle and turn back to the cookie room.

"Is she yours?" Shane points his glass at Abigail.

"She's Jenny's, but I'm her legal guardian."

Shane nods and almost seems sad for a moment. I didn't think he cared much, but I guess he must've had some fondness for our family to carry on a conversation with my dad this long after all this time.

"So, you and Sloan reconnected after all these years. Funny what happens in life."

"Yeah, it was surprising. I'm glad though."

"You two were pretty good friends."

"More than that," I say before I can stop myself. "Sloan was my best friend. It wasn't hard to pick up where we left off."

"Is that what's happening? Picking up friendship again?" He smirks, but I'm not sure it's the happy kind. "Or is it more?"

The back of my neck heats, my skin feels too tight. Recognizing that Shane isn't thrilled with the idea isn't difficult. His voice is riddled in a dark timbre.

He leans against the doorframe of the cookie room when I say nothing and takes a slow drink. "I understand," he tells me. "Old feelings come back, yet it's new and exciting at the same time."

"But?" I say in a sort of challenge.

He grins. "I tried for quite a few years to get Sloan out of this town. She excelled at the academy, excelled in college, and now look at all this. Her potential doesn't live here in Silver Creek, Rowan. I know you care about her, and would want the best for her. It's not here."

I clear my throat, hating how I let every word sting, as though he knows right where to press to draw out the same worries I've had myself. "With all due respect, Mr. Hanson," I start slowly. "Sloan is her own woman. She can decide what's best for her without my help, and without yours."

"She already has." A second voice comes at my back.

Sloan's ex, what's his name, stands behind me. Without her.

"Rowan," Shane says. "You met Luke."

The guy who cheated on her, yeah, we met. I'd like to say it, but instead I simply nod and force myself to shake the guy's hand.

"I don't mean to interrupt," Luke says. "But you ought to know, Sloan has already made her choice. The owner of this place has offered her a fulltime position in Utah. It's her dream job, and she's earned it after her work here." Luke tilts his head. "Surely she told you. She's leaving day after tomorrow to get started. I was just with her talking to Mark Bridger about it."

"She is rather excited," Shane says to Luke.

"Yeah, especially after Bridger told her the starting salary," Luke laughs. "Heck, maybe I'll try to steal the job from her."

They have a good laugh, while my stomach turns to lead. Sloan never mentioned a new job. A permanent job, hundreds of miles away. She never mentioned leaving for good. Again. Not that I trust either of them, but it does make sense that after the lodge was completed Sloan would have another position set up. I'm an idiot for allowing myself to forget that Sloan Hanson does not live here. She came for a little while, and eventually would need to go home. Naively I have lived over these ten days as if each day would be the same. Wake up, and Sloan would be there.

But she won't. The fantasy needed to end eventually.

I scan the crowd for Sloan, and catch her talking with my dad by the fireplace. Longing builds in my chest, sharp and deep.

"Rowan, you all right?" Shane asks. "At least you two will be able to keep in touch this time.'

"Yeah," I say quickly, eyes on the back of Sloan's head. My mind is whirling, searching for a solution, a way to keep this new normal. Everything about her is glowing when she turns around and I see her face, her smile, her eyes. I want her more than I've ever wanted a woman.

I love her.

I might lose her.

"This is a good opportunity for her?" I ask at Shane.

He nods, eyeing me with a touch of curiosity. "This has been her goal since graduate school. To run her own department, her own team."

Okay. I need to unravel this knot of upheaval I'm planning. I refuse to lose Sloan, and I refuse to stand in her way. I wouldn't do that. The trouble is meshing together two lives who've lived apart.

"I know, I get it. Sloan is like a unicorn. Hard to pin down," Luke says clapping me on the shoulder.

I think Shane tries to hush him. I suppose that's decent of her dad, but Luke goes on without care.

"Look, I'm sure you guys had your fun for a few days, but now it's time to go back to real life. Don't you think? You can see Sloan lives in a different world now and she doesn't need any distractions."

I scoff and shake him off my shoulder. "Sloan is not a unicorn. She's a woman and she deserves more than being pinned down. And I'd never try to hold her back. I just planned to love her. A lot better than you did. She's worth more than the way you treat her."

Luke steps back as if I've scalded him.

I glance at Shane. "If Sloan asks, would you tell her I stepped out? Excuse me."

"Rowan," her dad tries, but I've heard plenty.

I slip into the cookie room and tap my mom's shoulder. "I need to go for a second. Keep an eye on Abigail for me?"

"Ro, what's wrong?"

"I just gotta go."

My mom doesn't press, but I can feel her eyes on me across the lobby, until I'm outside, the lights of the Moosehead lodge at my back.

Chapter 19

Sloan

"Mom, have you seen Rowan?" I ask. It's not like he's hard to miss, towering over everyone as he does.

"Sloanie he left," Loo answers instead. "I don't know if something happened at the inn, or what, but he just high-tailed it out of here."

My stomach turns. "He left?" Why didn't he say anything? "Mom, what's with the face?"

She's glaring and gripping her hot chocolate mug a little too tightly if you ask me. I follow her dagger eyes across the room. My dad is muttering something to Tracy. Luke is standing by them both, a grimace shadowing his countenance like he might scream or punch something.

"Rowan was talking to your dad," my mom whispers. "Then he left."

"You're kidding." My fists clench at my sides. Without another word, I weave through the crowd, eyes homed in on my targets, and they *are* my targets. If they've done or said something to Rowan, I'll lose it. I don't care who sees.

My dad catches my eyes. Oh, this is rich—he looks nervous. He *did* say something.

"Sloan—"

"What did you say to Rowan? He left."

"Sloan keep your voice down," Tracy snaps.

"This is between me and my father," I clap right back.

"Sloan enough," Luke says. "He couldn't handle knowing you were taking the Alpine job, that's all. Guess he got all bent out of shape knowing you wouldn't play housewife with him."

My mouth drops and I gape at my dad. "Are you serious? You told him about Alpine?"

"The question is, why didn't you?" Luke answers and I'm starting to think there is something more in that eggnog.

"Go away, Lucas."

He hates his full name, and it seems to do the trick. With a roll of his eyes he sips his drink and saunters back into the meat of the party.

"Dad," I say, my voice breaks. "Why do you always interfere? Why do I embarrass you so much that you think you always need to intervene?"

"Sloan," Tracy gasps. "Watch your—"

"Tracy," I wheel on her. "I'm twenty-five, not a teenager anymore. Let me speak to my father."

She looks to my dad for his support, I guess, but he doesn't give it. He meets my eyes and rests his hand on the small of my back. "Let's go talk."

We don't go far, just on the other side of the wide fireplace, but there is enough seclusion I feel as though we can speak privately. My dad leans against the stone mantle and watches the party for a long moment before he looks at me. "You don't embarrass me, Sloan."

I roll my eyes. "You have a funny way of showing it. Why did you dump all the Alpine stuff on Rowan, tonight? I wanted to have a nice holiday with him, with mom, even with you and Hallie."

"I thought you wanted the Alpine position?"

"Yeah, so did I," I say meekly. "But now I realize, I did only because you wanted me to have it. Because you, and Luke, and Tracy, and Mark Bridger, told me it was perfect for me. That this is the life I want. You hear all that enough, and eventually you start to believe other people know best."

"Come on Sloan," he says. "You can't tell me a couple days with your old friend made you want to shift your entire life around. He's got a kid. He can't just travel around with you."

"No," I say, my chest tight. Each breath hurts. "But that doesn't give you, or Luke, the right to meddle in my relationships. I'm going to talk with him."

"Sloan don't be emotional. You're needed here," he tells me. "These aren't decisions you should make because of a fling, or whatever this is."

"It isn't a fling," I say, hating the way tears drip down my cheeks. People are starting to stare now. "I loved Rowan when you made me move eight years ago, and I love him now. Please, let me live my life, and trust that you and mom raised me well enough to make good decisions. What more will it take to prove that to you?"

"I am proud of you." The words come quickly; I nearly miss them.

I stop, utterly stunned.

My dad closes the space between us. "I'm proud of you, I've always been proud of you. Obviously, I should've said it more. All I've ever wanted is for you to see what you're capable of. Maybe I pushed too hard."

I take a deep breath. "I owe a lot of my accomplishments to you, Dad, but sometimes it would've been nice to know that I was okay just being your daughter."

"Sloan don't throw your goals away for anyone else. The one who cares about you won't ask you to do that."

"True," I say softly. "Good thing Rowan has never asked me to give up anything."

I turn away from him and hurry to the front of the lodge, grab my coat, and leave into the gilded lights and snowdrifts.

This feels too familiar, life trying to tear Rowan Graham away, him walking away, me left alone without knowing what will happen next.

I wipe a tear from the corner of my eye as I start my SUV. One thing I know—this time, I'm not going to stand there crying while I watch Rowan walk away. And if he wants me to, well then, he'll need to come up with a heck of an argument to get me out of his life a second time.

The inn is quiet when I arrive. Most of the guests are home for Christmas, and those who aren't are either hidden in their rooms or out on the town.

Lights are dim inside. Only the soft, cheerful glow of Christmas brightens my path to the dining room. Rowan isn't there. He isn't at the front desk. I check in the living room. The fire is lit and presents are stacked beneath the tree. When I turn to check upstairs, I note the light beneath the door of his office.

My steps are heavy, and I'm not sure if I'm furious with him for dashing away, or desperate to feel his arms around me with promises that nothing will change. At the door I knock once, then push my way inside.

Rowan is tucked behind an office desk, his laptop open, the screen lighting his face. His eyes flick to me, then back to the screen. "Hi. You shouldn't have left."

I play with one of my earrings and start to pace. "I could say the same to you. Funny, but this feels a little like another Christmas Eve I'd like to forget. I know my dad and Luke told you about my job offer." *Curse you tears.* My voice breaks. I'm fumbling to say everything while terrified this will turn out like a vicious repeat of eight years ago. "I had plans to talk to you about everything, but what really irritates me is you."

He lifts a brow and leans away from his computer. "Me?"

"Yes you," I snap. "I thought when you took the time to explain things about Abigail, when you told me how you really felt that night, I thought you wouldn't be the guy who walked away again."

"Sloan—"

"No," I say, taking a swifter pace around his office, my heart in my throat. "I need to say this. There are things people want for me, things I wanted for myself, and honestly no one else fit in the plan, especially not a grumpy innkeeper and an eight-year-old. But you happened, and turned everything upside down." I stop pacing and face him. "You reminded me of what I truly wanted, what I've always wanted. I love you Rowan Graham, and I always have. So don't you dare run away from me again."

I swat a tear away. Every inch of me is hot, and tight, and my blood rushes to my head. Rowan studies me until it feels as though every wall is crushing me. I blink rapidly, loosening my lashes of the salty tears. He pushes away from his desk after a few minutes, and sits on the corner.

"There are some things about what you said I take issue with," he says slowly, but his eyes are bright. "First, I'm not grumpy."

"You are. Sometimes." I wipe my cheek again.

He palms my hip, fingers gently sliding up my spine. I don't breathe when he shoots me with a sly grin. "Agree to disagree. Second, Abigail will insist you say that she's nine. But it's the last part that is really getting to me. The *don't run away* part."

"Oh, not the three words I said before?" I say through a snort. I told the man I loved him, and here I am waiting like a supplicant for the same, or the swift, wretched letdown if he doesn't.

His hand splays over my spine, urging me closer. His voice goes low. "We'll get to that." Rowan positions me between his knees. I rest my hands on his legs, our foreheads falling together as one of his hands cups the side of my face. "I'm not running from you, Sloan. I'm trying to keep you. I left to do a bit of research, and wasn't planning on being gone long, but I'm glad you're here since you know the market better than me. What do you think I could get for this place?"

I pull back. "What? You're not selling the inn."

"I can," he says. "If this job is your dream, I will."

"Rowan, you have Abigail."

He nods. "Yeah. Moving is scary for kids, but she'll make tons of friends again. Besides, she's mentioned more than once how she wishes we lived closer to my parents."

"Saying it and actually leaving her house are two different things."

"Yes, and never seeing a woman she's come to admire would be just as upsetting. We can do this."

"But . . ." He'd sell the inn to *follow* me? "But what will you do?"

He wraps his arm tightly around my waist, grinning. "Innkeeper isn't my only skill. I do have a degree in business. But I kind of like the idea of mooching off you. I could take up gaming and stay in my boxers all day, eating junk until I get a gut."

I smile and shake my head. "I am not your sugar mama." I close my eyes. "Why would you sell this place?"

His smile fades as he stands from the desk, his hands never falling away from my skin. The dark brown of his eyes simmers in a needy heat, his mouth is close. “If I could go back to that night, when a dumb kid walked away from you, I would hit him upside the head and tell him to wake up. I’m not walking away now, not ever again, because I am lost to you.”

A little gasp escapes my throat when his lips brush mine. I don’t say anything, not wanting to miss a word.

“I love you Sloan, all of you. I love your passion, your kindness, your ideas. You are who I hope Abigail wants to be, a strong” – he kisses my cheek – “smart” – my opposite cheek. I sigh. “funny” – his lips brush my forehead – “beautiful woman. I love you; definitely longer than you’ve loved me.”

“Are we going to have a competition because I’ll win.”

He grins and shakes his head. “I’m done talking.”

Rowan kisses me and I’m no longer in control. My body melts against his, my fingers in his hair. Each kiss slides to the next. I’m breathless and shift to be closer, but even pressed against him I feel too far apart. The rough stubble of his face, the way his hands hold me steady, keeping me close, all of it sends my head spinning in a perfect storm and at the center is this man, grounding me. Loving me.

I dip my chin to break apart. We breathe heavily, hands digging into each other, wanting the moment to go on. “Don’t sell this place.”

“We can figure it out—”

"I don't want to leave," I whisper. "Not unless you really want to."

He sits back slightly. "Sloan don't give up what you want. I'm not asking you to do that."

"But I don't want it," I say, the truth after so long. "Luke wanted it, my dad wanted it, I wanted to please them." He looks at me like he doesn't believe me, drawing a laugh from my throat. "I'm serious. I don't want to work for Mark Bridger, or move again when Silver Creek has always been home to me. I just forgot that for a little while."

"But all your work . . . I don't want you to regret—"

I press my fingers to his lips, drawing him into a quiet. "I want this. More than I've ever wanted anything. To be here, with you, with Abby. I still have my ambition, Mr. Graham, which is why you're going to hire me. I have ideas, you see, for this old place."

He chuckles, pressing a kiss to the tips of my fingers. "Really?"

"Big plans. I'm expensive, so be ready to pay up, but I promise you will be wowed."

"Trust me," he says in a rough voice as he tilts my face to his. "You take my breath away, being wowed by you will never be a problem."

When he kisses me again our movements are slow and gentle. No reason to rush, I think with a smile against his lips. We have all the time in the world.

Chapter 20

Sloan

Four months later

Summer is coming. I even wore shorts all day; Abigail cracked a few windows to let in the fresh mountain air. Something about Silver Creek in spring is a bit magical. But today is even better. The Holly Berry inn is jam packed with faces we love. My mom drove up from Boulder for the weekend. My dad—crazy as this sounds—let Hallie come stay for her Spring Break, and Rowan's parents decided to visit since Easter is this Sunday.

Even better than all that, I get to steal away a sexy innkeeper for a date tonight.

It's been too long. When winter ended, the outdoorsman came like flies. Fishermen desperate to spend lazy days on the lake, hikers, campers. All week, Rowan has been a ghost. Not that I just sit around. No, as the manager of the inn, thank you very much, I've had plenty of work to meet the demand. Jeri begged me for new appliances in the kitchen, stating I am the reasonable one on the team and Rowan would have her cooking over an open fire pit if it saved money. She hasn't stopped kissing my feet when I used my fancy contacts at the appliance depot and scored a double oven and twin dishwashers. Not to mention the massive refrigerator she's getting next week. It's large enough I could climb inside.

When Rowan and I do steal a few seconds alone, sometimes he'll ask me if I ever think about what life would be if I took the Alpine job. I think he keeps asking it because I always answer by kissing him, slow and fierce.

I've never looked back.

Not when Luke called and told me I was being ridiculous, then proceeded to leave voicemails after that when I wouldn't answer. Not when my dad sent me an email saying the position was still open, at least as of late February, and Mark Bridger seemed anxious to have me join the team. I certainly didn't look back when Tracy called and said I'd always be scrimping and struggling if I lived like a hermit in the mountains.

Judging the volume of voices in the living room from all the laugher and conversation, we are anything but hermits.

"Wear these ones," Hallie says as she holds a pair of silver earrings to her ears.

"No these," Abigail says, taking a pair of aqua studs.

Both girls are on their bellies over my mattress, making a mess of every piece of jewelry. I'm kind of obsessed with how they've become friends, though. Hallie is three years older, but Abigail is still taller and they could both live outside, climbing the trees and playing in the creek.

"I'm going with the diamond studs," I say as I finish glossing my lips.

Abigail sits up on her knees. "Are those real?"

"Uh, we'll pretend they are?"

She giggles and smacks Hallie in the shoulder. "Come on, Nana wants us to hurry."

"Have fun on girls' night," I call after them as they scurry out the door. Loo and my mom promised to take the girls to pizza and a movie, but really I think it's so Devin can have a break with his lungs without feeling like he's not participating.

"Have fun kissing," Hallie says and smooshes her lips together, making terribly wet noises. Abigail snickers.

"Oh, Hal, trust me," I say with a smirk. "I will."

She rolls her eyes and mutters, "gross," under her breath before running down the stairs after Abigail.

With one final glance in the mirror I smile, my stomach flips in the best ways, and I hurry out of my room. Rowan is leaning over the front desk. The black T-shirt he wears hugs all his divots and tone in ways that make it impossible not to reach out and touch the man. From behind, I wrap my arms around his waist, pressing my cheek against the warmth of his back. I love the way his laugh rumbles deep in his chest.

"Ready to be alone for more than two seconds."

He adjusts, so we're chest to chest and follows my lead by curling his arms around my body. I lift my chin, pointing my mouth toward his and hum a little. "So ready. What are we doing?"

"You're going to love it," he says, and pokes his head into the living room. "Abs, listen to Nana."

"Bye!" her voice shouts back.

Rowan slips his fingers into mine and we leave before anything can keep us from going on this date. It's happened before. On the way out, something will leak, or a guest needs the first aid kit, or the power goes out. I'm determined to be long gone before anything takes the night away.

"What's the plan?" I ask once we're on Main Street. I nestle close to his side in the truck, the way I always do, one palm on his leg. "You never said."

He grins, wide and bright. "We're going to become true Silver Creek Seniors."

I bark a laugh. "You're kidding? You are taking me to make-out on the fifty-yard line?"

"Uh, yes. And since we're old now, we'll beat the teenagers. We probably want to leave by eleven though. Kids get desperate to get their spot."

I shake my head. "You're weird."

"Why? We made plans to give each other the title, I'd say it's time we see it through."

"You're honestly telling me you didn't go with some other girl after I moved?"

His forehead wrinkles. "You think I'd let someone else take your spot? No way."

I rest my head on his shoulder. "Good answer."

The high school parking lot is empty when we arrive. A few outside lights brighten the way to the field at the back, and it feels delightfully juvenile to be here after all this time with Rowan. The one boy who I always wanted to take me here. We pass through the paved space near the bleachers, but when I see the grass, I freeze.

Along the fifty-yard line are flickering candles in small vases, and scattered arrangements of daisies, my favorite flower. Rowan grins shyly and squeezes my hand, urging me to follow. My feet are heavy, my palm feels sweaty in his. I can't swallow right, not with my heart stuck in the back of my throat.

"Rowan," I say in a rasp. "What is this?"

"I thought we'd do this in style," he tells me as we step onto the center of the line.

I shudder when his fingers trace the line of my jaw, his other arm curls around my waist. A burn builds behind my eyes when he kisses me sweet and raw.

"Sloan," he says, voice rough. "I love you, and there's something incredibly important I need to ask you."

I know it's coming, but even still, when Rowan takes my hands in his and lowers to the damp grass on his knee, I swallow three hiccups to keep from choking on a swell of emotion. He smiles at me, his eyes simmering with a touch of gold from the candles.

"Sloan Marie Hanson," he says slowly. "You are my best friend; you've always been my best friend. You stole my heart a long time ago, and even if it took us a while to get here, I want you to have it forever. I want you, day after day, always. So, will you marry me?"

"It's about time," I say in a breathy gasp before dropping to my knees and crushing my lips to his. My arms squeeze around his neck as I kiss him, one easing into the next, before I pull back and whisper, "Yes, I will marry you. Tomorrow, now, I don't care."

At that I hear the screaming and cheering. Rowan laughs as Abigail and Hallie squeal on the bleachers, jumping on their toes as they dart across the field. My mom is sniffing and wiping her face, trying to hold her phone to record us, I assume. Loo and Devin hold hands and rush us after the girls. Even Jeri and Gifford came holding balloons and laughing with our families.

It turns into a pass around night of hugs and kissing and planning and screaming. But when a moment of quiet comes, I look at Rowan in the candlelight, take his face between my hands and whisper that I'll love him forever.

But the truth is, since that day on the slides when I met my best friend, I've always loved Rowan Graham.

And I always will.

Rowan

CHRISTMAS FUTURE--THREE YEARS FROM NOW

"Wake up lazy bones!" I steamroll over Abigail's skinny body still buried in her bedspread.

She groans and tries to kick at me. "Dad, you aren't supposed to be waking me up! That's supposed to be me."

I don't really know when she stopped calling me Uncle Rowan and started tossing out Dad, it sort of became a natural thing we just slipped into once she became mine permanently.

Well, ours. Sloan took to being called Mom like it was something that had always been. I poke at Abigail's hip and stick my cell phone underneath her little tent of bedsheets. "It's seven in the morning, kid. Who sleeps in this late on Christmas morning?"

"Ugh," she says dramatically; she's giggling too. "You're such a weirdo."

"We're starting without you and I don't know, like maybe, like there is, like a cool cell phone or something in one of the, like, boxes."

Abigail tosses back her quilt, jolting straight up in bed. "Are you serious?"

I shrug. "Eh, I doubt it."

She glares at me, but the childlike gleam is still there in her eyes, as much as she pretends being *almost* twelve means she's fully independent and has no need of parents. I don't need to coax her much more to get her out of bed and hurrying down the stairs. That's what I love, seeing her so excited she might burst. But on the other hand, I have a healthy distaste for how she's getting old enough that she's not pouncing on me at five in the morning anymore.

Downstairs the inn is quiet, all the guests checked out last night, and we have until tomorrow before anyone else is scheduled to check back in. Jeri is with her mom and cousins in San Diego this year, and Kristine and my parents aren't due to come until this afternoon. I'm interested to see how this year goes. Shane is coming to bring Hallie up tomorrow. She's going to spend the rest of Christmas break with us, and Shane will stay for two days. While Kristine is still here.

They keep it pleasant for Sloan and Hallie's sake, but at this point it would be a Christmas miracle if there wasn't tension between my in-laws.

Abigail barrels into the living room where a fire is already chasing away the chill, and the same mismatched, blue, silver, red and green Christmas tree is bright and ready to be plucked. We kept the same ornaments from that first year Sloan and I found each other again. Seems wrong to change it.

"Finally." Sloan stands in the center of the room, wearing flannel pajamas, her curly hair a little wild, and hands on her hips. "Kiddo, something is wrong when the parents are begging the kid to open to presents."

Abigail hugs her quickly before plopping onto the floor and staring hungrily at the tree.

Sloan clicks her tongue and pulls down the stockings. "These first."

Abigail is halfway through her stocking when Sloan nestles against my side on the loveseat and kisses my jaw. I tug her in close as we start to go through our gifts and stockings.

With just the three of us, unwrapping gifts doesn't take too long. Abigail's focus was suctioned away when, in fact, she was gifted a phone. I still think it's too young, but she is on a competition dance team this year and will be taking a few out of town trips. Sloan made a good argument. I mean, it doesn't even do all the normal things our phones do, and Abigail has said thank you no less than one hundred times, even after we laid out all the rules.

I love how she's grinning ear to ear. But still. I wish the gift debates were still over Barbie dolls or bracelet kits.

Sloan slides off the couch and ruffles around the gifts left for our parents that we'll open tonight until she drags out a small box. She smiles at me.

"Here, this is the last one."

"What is this?" I ask, taking it from her gently. "You've officially gotten more for me than I got for you. And we agreed, wife, that we wouldn't out buy each other."

She chuckles. "Well, husband, this one is sort of a family gift."

Abigail snuggles next to Sloan at that. I've never been one to enjoy being the center of attention, so it's a little unnerving having both women in my life staring at every move I make.

The box is small, tied in a neat little bow, and when I lift the lid, I'm confused for a moment. Two socks are inside. Little socks. Baby socks.

Baby socks.

My mouth parts. My eyes pop when I spin around, so I'm looking at Sloan. Oh, great. Oh, great. Her eyes have tears in them. Abigail has her hands over her mouth. She's bouncing on the couch.

"Wait," I say, a little breathless. I rest one hand on Sloan's leg. "Wait, what is this? Sloan, are you—are you—"

"Kiddo number two," she whispers as she laces her fingers with mine.

"We're having a baby!" Abigail shouts and hugs her mom.

I'm stunned. I don't move.

"Rowan," Sloan says, curling her arms around my waist. "Your mouth is open."

"A baby," I say. My throat is tight. There is a sting behind my eyes, and nothing I could say seems adequate.

A furrow forms between Sloan's brows. "Are you happy?"

I cough, I guess to get my words flowing. When I look at her, she's blurry, but I smile through a croaky laugh. "Happy?" Instead of answering, I buy some time by pulling her mouth to mine. I kiss her until she understands all the beautiful, perfect things I'm feeling all at once. I kiss her until Abigail groans and tells us to get a room like a solid tween.

"Sloan," I say when I finally break apart. "I am more than happy, there isn't a word to tell you what I'm feeling."

She flings her arms around my neck and holds me tightly. Abigail pretends to be disgusted, but I notice the way she smiles.

I point at her. "Why wouldn't I want a baby when I have a built-in babysitter."

Abigail tosses tissue paper at us, but hurries to the couch. "You better pay up then." She laughs and wraps her arms around both of us. We curl her into our embrace. "I'm can't wait to be a sister," Abigail whispers.

I hug both my girls tighter. I kiss Abigail on the head, kiss Sloan on the lips once more. I thought the Christmas that Sloan strolled back into my life would be the one I'd hold at the top of important Christmases.

But here, with my daughter, my wife, and a new baby on the way—I can't imagine anything better than this Christmas, than this moment. Ever.

Christmas at the Cafe

Sneak Peek

Jeri

There are signs to watch for when you know you've just become a Christmas hero.

When another human walks into a perfectly scented room of vanilla, cinnamon, and a hint of clove. They breathe through the nose. The eyes roll back in the head. One

of the key signs. More important than words. The final one—the sigh and coinciding grin.

When those come, I know I've basically entered sainthood in this old inn's kitchen.

"Jeri, it smells amazing." Sloan says.

She tucks a lock of her pale hair behind her ear, and goes through the checklist in

about point two seconds.

With a long stride, Sloan crosses to the island countertop in the cozy kitchen. It's been remodeled recently, but since the Holly Berry Inn is over one hundred years old, Sloan kept a vintage feel while updating the appliances at the same time. I don't know how she does it. But the woman is a master at marketing and ambiance. Some of us master settings, some of us cook. Call me a hippie, but I'd say Sloan Graham is an artist all on her own.

"What time did you get here?" she asks.

"About five," I say, grinning. It never gets old, someone reveling in the scents and tastes that come from my hands.

Sloan holds a hand over her slender middle, a bit of the pallid greenness in her cheeks fades the longer she snorts up the steam from the sweet rolls on the cooling rack. I'll swear to my dying breath there is a glisten of tears in her eyes.

"I don't feel sick," she says, voice rough. "If I can just bottle this smell up, I think I'll survive this."

I laugh and give her shoulders a squeeze. "You'll survive, but I know for sure this little nugget is Rowan's kid since he-she is already causing so much trouble."

Sloan sniff-laughs. A new thing with my sassy, take-names friend. A few months ago, Sloan was not the woman who crumbled over a breakfast food. Lately, she's either crying, eating, or laughing at anything. It's spinning Rowan's head because everyone knows that man lives to make this woman smile and if he can't do that—he starts to panic.

Good. Rowan is still my moody innkeeper buddy, and after watching him grumble through life, I think he deserves the head spin. Even if hormones are a little wild up in here, he smiles more than anyone now.

She goes in for another deep inhale, snorting and groaning on her way up. "Mmm. What is that? These are not typical sweet rolls."

No. No they aren't. I might be a small-town chef, but I am one of those culinary weirdos who view food as a solid artform. It's expressive, it's creative, it's an escape.

"I added a bit of cardamom and clove. Just a hint of nutmeg in the icing, too. I'm
impressed, Sloanie. Not everyone catches the changes."

"I have the nose of a blood hound lately. It's a curse more than anything." She
rests her cheek on the edge of the countertop, ogling the fresh rolls from the
side. "I think I'm in love with you."

Sloan's lip quivers. I'm not sure she even realizes it. I nudge her shoulder. "Girl, no
worries. I'll come bake these bad boys every morning until munchkin comes."

"No. No, you don't need to do all this. We have the casseroles, and some freezer
things. Plus, Angel is really getting a feel for the kitchen. Jer, you've got your own café now and—"

"Sloan," I interrupt. "I know, but I still want to help out here until Angel feels
totally comfortable. Besides, it's Christmastime. Busy season. I'll help."

She laughs. "Sometimes I wish I could use my sign the door opens so much."

I glance at the chic chalkboard in the corner that reads, *Sorry, no room at the inn.*

One of those things that made Sloan laugh way too hard.

Holly Berry Inn has exploded since Sloan came back into Rowan's life. Childhood

friends, reunited into lovers. Three Christmases ago, I basically had a front row seat to their delightful love story, and it's been a blast ever since.

Sloan has worked with massive resorts, setting up staff, opening them, marketing. She's made Holly Berry a true mountain escape without ripping away the

rural feel.

Rowan even hired staff. He *never* planned for staff. I swear, for years I thought the man would turn into the town hermit and stop talking all together.

But no, now on the grounds of Holly Berry there are new faces to keep up with

maintenance, the stables, clean rooms, check-in guests. Enough, I was able to

turn over the head chef position to a new, amazing baker and open my own café.

A longtime dream.

Still, it's hard to ditch Holly Berry completely. I'm sentimental, that's all.

I reach for my messenger bag, and beanie, taking a minute to enjoy the look of pure satisfaction on Sloan's face for another breath.

"I'm going to head out," I say. "If Angel gets swamped, let me know—"

"We won't."

"Rude."

She grins. "Because The Pot is swamped as much as we are. Go. You've saved my morning. You're my hero. I love you and need you."

"It should be awkward hearing my wife declare love to you," comes a deep, soothing timbre. "But it's just the norm now."

Rowan comes in the back door, shoulders dusted in a layer of fresh powder, carrying a stack of chopped wood. The guy is a mountain man. Bushy black beard, but still kempt. Flannel coat, handsome broody face.

Sloan goes to him, and I'm pretty sure she sniffs him to make sure her stomach can handle it, then kisses him.

"You'll always be my top lover love, but Jeri . . . she's a close, *close* second."

I roll my eyes, and secure my knit hat over my caramel chocolate hair. It's how my Nana always described it. Dark and smooth with a touch of gold. Everything was food with Nana, though. People shouldn't wonder how I got into culinary arts.

"Later, you two. Keep the PDA to a minimum. You have an eleven-year-old girl who is starting to notice the boys on the playground. She's going to get ideas."

Rowan's jaw tightens. "Take it back, Jericho. Abs doesn't even know what a boy *is*."

Papa bear is my favorite thing to poke. And I do. Often. "Whatever you say, bud. See you later."

Sloan perks up. "Oh! Let me know how the new flavor goes."

I stop, a little stunned for a moment. My family isn't close. After Nana died, my only sister moved to Virginia and we talk maybe every three months. Love her, we're simply different.

But this, this is like the family I had growing up with my grandmother. That Sloan remembered I'm starting a new Christmas flavor today for the coffee and hot chocolate bar means something.

A curl tugs at the corner of my mouth.

"For sure," is all I say. Any more and I might start lip quivering like Sloan. The
Grahams, Holly Berry Inn, they're my family. Other than my food creations,
they're all I really need.

Silver Creek is a town right off a Christmas postcard. Nestled in the mountains of
Colorado, it's been my home for the last decade and I have no plans on leaving.
Small, rural, cozy. A place where neighbors wave even if they don't recognize
you. Where everyone knows everything about everyone, and scandal is discussed
over café tables or hairdresser seats.

Not without its quirks, but during the holidays it's magical.

Sidewalk shops are trimmed in real evergreen wreaths, their windows are painted in
festive scenes. Each lamppost is wrapped in white fairy lights, so when the sun
sets this town becomes part of another world. Red, heavy bows are tied all along the iron park fence, and along the edges are snow flecked houses with Christmas scenes behind the windows. Elves, turkey dinners, Christmas

morning,

Santa sneaking down the chimney.

I grin at a few parents pausing to show their little kids the scenes as grownups

chat over coffee and hot chocolate from Stan Willy's annual holiday food truck

parked on the street.

With every gust of wind hints of pine spice and smoke fill my lungs. I breathe a

little deeper. The fresh snow on the walks is blinding, but I hate covering any

of the morning with sunglasses. I love this time of year. Busy as it is, I live for this town and this season.

Call it a bit of a holiday stupor for my lack of attention. If I'd been tuned in to

my surroundings I might not have taken the sidewalk that wraps around the back

of my café. If I hadn't walked around the back of my café, I might've avoided

the rogue ice ball.

Then again, if I avoided the ice ball, what came after might never have happened.

One minute I'm absorbing all the spicy, sparkly goodness of Silver Creek, and the next the left side of my face is on fire. Full on burning in flames. It's the only way to explain it. Black spots dot the corners of my eyes. From my temple to the hinge of my jaw prickles in sharp, white-hot pain.

I stumble. A high voice, one that cracks as if it can't decide if it wants to be high or low, calls my name. I'm not interested in the voice, I'm trying to stay upright. A lamppost is there to brace against. Without question I'm sliding like a fool, grappling for the iron. It feels as if my brain is throbbing against my skull as I try to steady my feet beneath me.

The door of the Honey Pot is five feet away, but it's not close enough.

The moment I realize my heel has hit the stupid plot of black ice I've been begging Trace, the guy responsible for salting the walks, to fix, is the moment when time comes to a crawl.

I'm aware my feet are not longer on the ground. My eyes are locked on the bright blue winter sky; it's almost comforting. Even if my brain knows I'm about to land smack on my back on the frosty sidewalk. My stomach drops to my knees.

Then, I hit.

Funny, but it doesn't hurt nearly as much as I thought. Don't get me wrong, my hips
are screaming, but my head didn't smack. My skull isn't smashed across the pavement. I don't even think I hit my head. No concussion for Christmas? I'd
say this is a win.

Still, I'm frozen in place. A snowdrift swallows my legs to my thighs, my rear is
soaked on the walk, but my shoulders and head are propped up. Why are my
shoulders and head propped like I'm sitting up in bed?

"Whoa, are you okay?"

A few flurries of snow sprinkle across my cheeks. I blink against the glare of
the sun into an unfamiliar—albeit gorgeous—face. The baseball hat pulled over
his brow shadows the color of his eyes, but if they are anything like the lower
lines and sharp edges, no doubt they're the sort of eyes that break into the soul.

Maybe I do have a concussion because I think my heart wants to fall in love.

Check out Christmas at the Café available on Amazon.

Want More?

In my digital books I always include a bonus scene. Now with a QR code you can have that bonus scene as a digital download on your phone or tablet. Enjoy a peek into Rowan and Sloan's happily ever after, plus receive a fun, festive holiday recipe. Scan the code below.

If you have any trouble, don't hesitate to reach out at em@emilycauthor.com and we'll get you squared away.

Also By Emily Childs

For Love and Rock

Our Secret Song

Our Broken Song

A Little Love

A Little Like Romeo

A Little Ado About Love

A Little Fool For You

The Debutante Rules

Don't Marry the Mechanic

Don't Marry the Enemy

Don't Marry the Ex

Don't Marry the Boss

Made in the USA
Las Vegas, NV
22 November 2023